IMPACT

THE DEAN CURSE CHRONICLES

STEVEN WHIBLEY

Published by Steven Whibley Publishing
Victoria, British Columbia
www.stevenwhibley.com

Publisher: Steven Whibley
Editing: Maya Packard
Copyediting: Maya Packard, Chandler Groover
Cover Design: Pintado (rogerdespi.8229@gmail.com)
Interior Layout and Design: www.tammydesign.ca

Library and Archives Canada Cataloguing in Publication

Whibley, Steven, 1978-
        Impact / Steven Whibley.

(Dean Curse chronicles)
Issued also in electronic format.
ISBN 978-1-927905-01-2 (bound).--ISBN 978-1-927905-00-5 (pbk.)
ISBN 978-1-927905-02-9 (pdf)

        I. Title. II. Series: Whibley, Steven, 1978- Dean Curse chronicles.

PS8645.H46I46 2014   jC813'.6   C2014-902451-7
                                                     C2014-902452-5

For Isaiah, and Aubree

– Steven Whibley

IMPACT

THE DEAN CURSE CHRONICLES

STEVEN WHIBLEY

CHAPTER 1

I was going to die.

Me, Dean Curse, the guy who knows when other people are going to die. You'd think having this power of premonition would mean I'd get a couple perks. You'd think I'd at least be able to save myself when the situation called for it—like it did right now.

From the other side of the couch, Rodney Palmer taunted, "Maybe you should start cursing, eh, Curse?" He laughed at his own pun and then added, "No, wait, you should start begging for mercy and then change your name to Dean Begs. How about that? Hmm?"

I rolled my eyes. I'd already heard every stupid joke possible about my name. I was tired of them. And tired of Rodney, too. His jokes sucked, and I would've told him so, except that Rodney was about the size of a gorilla, and just as predictable. Plus, he took up most of the couch, and every time things got heated on screen he'd shift and elbow me in the arm. I couldn't be sure he was doing it on purpose but it's not like he was known for his fair play.

I gripped my controller and narrowed my gaze at the

screen. I shot back at him, but missed, and he nailed me again. My life meter slipped into the red. Colin lifted his controller as he tried to get his guy behind Rodney's, but it was too late. Rodney's characters moved a lot faster in a game than Rodney did in real life.

My meter emptied. I died.

Well, the me in *Halo* croaked, that is.

I let my controller drop to my lap and flopped back on the big leather couch we were all sharing.

We were supposed to be in Dr. Mickelsen's therapy session working toward psychological healing after experiencing the school explosion that had killed my History teacher a few months ago. I didn't really feel like I got a lot out of therapy these days, but that was probably because my dad's a therapist, so I've learned to tune out anyone who uses the therapist tone on me. I also knew, though, that therapy could help a lot of people. It seemed to help Lisa. It might even help me if I could actually talk about stuff. What would I say, though?

Hey, Doc, remember that disaster at the museum a few weeks back? The one where an entire wing was destroyed and a giant T. rex skeleton was turned to rubble? That was me. Oh, and if I touch someone, I'll know when they're going to die—or at least, I'll know twenty-four hours before that they're going to die.

No, I couldn't say that. My best friends, Lisa and Colin,

were my partners, and they knew everything. I used them as my therapists.

Still, Lisa found Dr. Mickelsen helpful, and Colin and I were there for her ... Well, we'd intended to be there for her. Then we heard the game, found Rodney, and thought it was finally our chance to beat the giant bully at something. Who knew he was practically a *Halo* master?

Most of the time, Rodney hardly said anything. In fact, before this game, I'd been pretty sure he communicated like an ape, using gestures and grunts to get his points across. But once the onscreen killing started, the kid didn't shut up. He shouted at the screen, mocking my moves and those of my team. I figured that was the point of having a video game room in a therapist's office—to get kids talking. Clearly it worked for Rodney.

It was going to take a heck of a lot more than a video game to get me talking. Even if I thought the secret society I was part of—the Congregation of Sacrifice—would be okay with me telling a psychologist about them and how we all have the same ability, I still wouldn't do it because the doctors would lock me up. I know how crazy it sounds.

I leaned back on the couch as Colin struggled to keep his character alive a few seconds longer. I imagined going back in time to when my grades at school were the most important thing in my life. Or when my biggest problem was dealing with my bratty sister, Becky. Back before I had to deal with other people's life or death.

Life and death in a simple game? Easy. Reality, though? That's something totally different.

"Hey!" The shout had all of us jumping and turning. Eric Feldman stood in the doorway, hands on his hips like he was a hall monitor or something. Rodney dropped his controller, pushed off the couch, and slunk over to Eric's side. He took up a crossed-arm pose like he hadn't just been busted with us.

I stood up to face Eric. "What?"

"You guys probably didn't even sign in, did you? I bet Dr. Mickelsen would love to know you're in here playing games rather than in therapy." Eric turned and left. Rodney followed him, a giant shadow trailing after skinny Eric.

"What a punk," Colin muttered.

I tapped him on the arm. Colin's not only my best friend; he's also one of the nicest guys around. He has TVs the size of Dr. Mickelsen's in pretty much every room in his house. Even the kitchen. But he never brags about it.

I nodded toward the door. "Let's get to Mickelsen before Eric makes it all our fault and tells him we ..."

Too late. Eric, Rodney, and Dr. Mickelsen all showed up in the doorway.

Dr. Mickelsen's gray hair stood up like he hadn't combed it in weeks. Colin and I keep arguing over whether he dyes his beard black or not. How can you have gray hair like that and a black beard? He keeps it trimmed short, and you can tell when he's thinking about stuff because he starts to stroke the whiskers.

He wasn't rubbing it now. Eric's face twisted into a smug sneer. I wanted to punch him, but I knew that would just get Dr. Mickelsen talking about anger issues. Eric started to say something, but Dr. Mickelsen held up a hand. "Rodney, see if Lisa would like to join us. Maybe a game is just what we all need."

Eric deflated, and I really had to try not to laugh. Then I remembered we'd been coming to therapy to show our support for Lisa, and she'd been expecting us to come today and participate with everyone who was still going to the group sessions, and I suddenly felt really bad. Worse when she stepped into the room and gave us looks that said, *You picked a video game over me?*

I gave her a shrug, and Colin mouthed the words "ice cream later" at her. She plopped down in a big chair, folded her arms, and wouldn't look at us.

Dr. Mickelsen set us all up with controllers. Networked gaming was so cool that Colin's eyes lit up, and I almost forgot why we were there. We all played for about a half hour. Dr. Mickelsen was actually pretty good and destroyed everyone except Lisa. So it came down to the two of them in the end. Lisa threw a grenade, and *boom*, she won.

"So, what do you feel when you die in a game like this? Or when you see others die?" the doctor asked.
I glanced at Colin. He stared up at the ceiling tiles. Eric poked Rodney, who sat on his hands now.

Lisa shifted in her chair. "It's not the same. When Dean sees people who are going to—" She broke off what she'd been about to say and shook her head, her blond ponytail swaying. She'd pulled her feet out of her running shoes when she sat down, and now pushed her shoes under her chair with her toes. "You know, it's hard to see anyone hurt and not be able to help them. Or be too late."

"You're saying you have empathy for other people's emotions?" Dr. Mickelsen asked.

Rodney's face tightened. "Empathy?" The word came out like "emputty."

Eric snickered, but Dr. Mickelsen said, "It means you can feel the same thing as another person. You understand when someone else is happy or sad."

Rodney's face scrunched up even more, but Eric muttered under his breath, "Some people shouldn't have to die. Like Mrs. Farnsworthy—" Eric broke off. He sounded like he had trouble getting her name out. His eyes seemed really bright and shimmery, and I wondered if he'd cry. If he did, I'd give him an Academy Award for being the world's best actor. He was only still in therapy because he knew it would score him sympathy votes. I was sure of it. Okay, I was only pretty sure of it, but he was a jerk to everyone, so I wasn't about to feel sorry for him.

The mention of Mrs. Farnsworth, my old History teacher, created a knot in my stomach every time. I shifted on my chair. I didn't want to talk about her. She shouldn't have had to die; I had even had a vision about her death. But I didn't know what I was doing back then. I still don't. Not really.

No one said anything for a few minutes. Then Colin broke the silence. "I think this world would be too crowded if we all lived forever. And ... well, don't we learn more because other people lived and died before us?"

Dr. Mickelsen sat back in his chair. He stroked his beard. Uh-oh. "Have you been thinking about the past a lot?" he asked. "Does that interest in the past have something to do with your recent museum visits? I know you were there when they had their ... um ... problems. How do you feel about what happened over there?"

Colin's mouth hung open. I heard Lisa swallow from where I was sitting. My hands had gone cold. What did he mean, he knew we were there? No one knew we were there. If they did, we'd be in jail or juvenile detention or somewhere else locked up. Eric stared at us, his eyes narrowed like he somehow knew we were to blame for a lot of stuff and couldn't wait to prove it and get us in trouble. Rodney picked up a game controller and started to fiddle with the buttons.

Dr. Mickelsen just waited, staring at us. After a few awkward minutes, he spoke. "Our time's up for today. But I think it would be a good assignment, Dean, Colin, and Lisa, for the three of you to visit the museum again. Sometimes we need to find closure with our own past, and that means we need to revisit it. Write down your feelings after you stop by the museum, and we'll talk about them. Eric and Rodney, I've got another idea for you two."

"Shock therapy?" Colin asked, hopeful. He looked at Dr. Mickelsen but gestured to Eric and Rodney. "I bet they'd really benefit from that."

"And Colin would benefit from a full lobotomy," Eric snapped. He nudged Rodney with his elbow, and the goon leaned forward. One more nudge and I bet Eric had him trained to attack.

"Okay, that's enough," the doctor said. "But since we didn't get a ton of time with everyone today, I am going to make myself available in a few days for another session." I had to stifle the groan. "I'll let your parents know about it. And of course, we'll still have our regular meeting next week," he said, then gestured to me, Lisa, and Colin. "Have a good day, you three. And if you two," he said, looking at Rodney and Eric, "would hang back just a few moments ..."

I didn't wait for him to finish his sentence. He'd dismissed us, and I bolted for the door. Outside, Colin and

Lisa met up with me. I didn't know what Dr. Mickelsen's plans were for Eric and Rodney, but hoped it involved something really far away.

"What are we going to do?" Colin asked. "I mean, about the museum?"

"Uh, how about we avoid it," I said. "And find a way to avoid this extra session Mickelsen has planned for us."

Lisa tucked a stray strand of her hair back behind her ear. She folded her arms and looked from Colin to me. I realized the only reason we had the extra session was because Colin and I had opted for *Halo* over therapy, and worse, I'd just reminded Lisa of that fact.

"Sorry," Colin said first. "We were coming to therapy. We were on our way."

"But wanted to have a playdate with your new BFF first?" Lisa asked.

I imagined Rodney with one of those BFF necklaces on and laughed, then tried to cover it up with a cough. "We really are sorry."

Lisa shook her head. "I'm not mad. You guys don't need therapy. I totally do. Thanks for even coming that far. I don't mind the extra session. It's not that big of a deal. But I'm still pretty torn about what to do about the museum."

"Not you, too," I said. "We can't go back there. Even though they don't *know* it was us, we did wreck the place. I'd rather they never even thought about us again."

Lisa shrugged. "We also wrecked that T. rex."

"T. *wrecked*," Colin said and grinned at us.

I glanced at him and didn't smile. "I don't think they want us back at the museum."

Colin slapped us both on the back. "You guys. We saved people. We reunited a Cambodian village with their sacred relic, and we saved a Buddhist monk. Do you even realize the karma points we get for that? Besides, we're supposed to learn more about the Society, aren't we?"

I was as anxious as they were to learn more about the *Congregatio de Sacrificio*—the Congregation of Sacrifice, or CS. Ever since I'd found out my visions made me part of the group, I'd been dying to get a formal meet-and-greet with the rest of the members. But there'd been one delay after the next. But all that was going to change tomorrow morning. It was all set. We were meeting Archer at the mall and he was driving us to the headquarters. I was trying to be cool about the whole thing, but inside I was a five-year-old on Christmas Eve. I was pretty sure Colin and Lisa were as excited as me, and were trying to be cool about it too.

We didn't talk a ton during the walk home, and I tried to distract myself with good thoughts about the museum, not thoughts of what we destroyed, but what we'd saved—lives. We turned onto my street, and I kicked at a rock in my path. It flew up, and the next thing I heard was a loud, "Ouch!"

Looking up, I saw Rylee Davis.

She'd been standing on the sidewalk in front of my house. She seemed to have just been standing there, like she might have been waiting for me. She didn't have her bike with her or skates on or anything. She rubbed her arm and smiled when she saw me looking at her. My mouth dried. Colin snickered, and I jabbed an elbow into his side.

Lisa called out, "Hey, Rylee."

Rylee glanced at her and then looked back at me, almost like she hadn't even seen Lisa. The summer sun showed lighter streaks in Rylee's long dark hair. Standing next to Lisa, who usually wore running shoes and clothes that made it easier for her to climb trees, Rylee looked way more like a girly-girl. She had on a sleeveless dress with little flowers all over it. For some reason, her lips always looked wet, like she'd just eaten fresh watermelon. I didn't mind that. And I kind of liked her eyes. Green and soft like she was always smiling inside.

"Hi, Dean." She turned pink as she said my name.

I nodded and scuffed my running shoes on the sidewalk. I had no idea what she wanted. As far as I knew, she didn't live around here. She smiled again at me. Flutters shook my stomach, and I gave her a wave.

"Well, we'll see you guys tomorrow morning," I said, which was awkward because of course I wasn't going to see Rylee, and she knew it, so it was as if I was ignoring the fact she was there. I felt like such an idiot.

Lisa and Rylee waved back, and Colin gave me a *what are you doing?* look. I knew I should've talked to Rylee, but I just couldn't. I jogged inside, only glancing back as I stepped through the door—just in time to see Rylee's face fall.

Great. Way to make a lasting impression, Dean.

CHAPTER 2

My alarm went off and I leaped out of bed. Finally, I'd meet the other members of the Society. Finally I'd get to know others who lived with the same ability as me. I'd have people who understood what it was like, people to give me advice and teach me things that would make my crazy life easier to deal with.

I showered and threw on some clean clothes. I knew Lisa and Colin would be as eager as me, and they'd be on their way if they weren't already waiting in the kitchen. I felt too nervous to eat but thought a piece of toast might settle the butterflies a bit, so I took the stairs two at a time, rushed into the kitchen, and slammed smack into my sister, Becky. She gave a shriek, and the box she'd been carrying went flying, scattering white bits into the air. I reached for the box with one hand and saved Becky from a fall with my other hand.

Instead of thanking me, Becky set up a howl. "Look at what you did!"

"Uh, what?"

I looked up and saw my parents staring at us from the

living room. I turned back to my sister, put her on her feet, and dumped the white bits back into the shoebox she was cradling. "You're collecting plastic now?"

Becky scowled and then kind of smirked like she had a secret. I glanced down at one of the white bits that had stuck to my sweaty palm. The shape looked foreign at first, and then I recognized it. "Oh, no—no! Tell me this is not what I think it is."

"Okay, it's not what you think it is."

"It's a tooth!" I slapped the tooth off my hand and wiped my palm on my T-shirt to get the ick off it. "That's someone's tooth. Why on earth do you have a box of teeth?"

Becky huffed out a breath. "This is a serious comparative study of bone density and ..."

She started yakking on and on about stuff. She's eleven and talks like she should be in college already. I jerked around to look at my dad, who was sitting in a chair across the room. "Are you seriously going to tell me this is normal?" I pointed at my sister. "C'mon, Dad, if this isn't a warning sign that she'll grow up to be a psychopath, I don't know what is."

My dad placed the magazine he was reading on his lap and folded his hands on top of it. He fixed me with his professional psychologist look, the one that's way too patient and understanding. "It's entirely normal, Dean." He smiled at Becky. "It's an imaginative collection, sweetheart. It's also very interesting you were able to get so many pieces from online auction sites."

Imaginative?

To be fair, my dad started out working with criminals who probably collected human heads. His idea of "normal" might have been seriously skewed.

But Mom chimed in, sounding all too cheerful. "Not many people have collections like that."

I shook my head. "Yeah, there's a reason for that. She has a box of teeth. Human teeth!"

"They're not all human," Becky said, sticking out her chin.

I sucked in a lungful of air and kept my stare on my folks. "Do you know who else collects stuff that weird? People who make suits out of human skin! And cannibals. Cannibal serial killers."

Mom's mouth tightened. "That's enough, Dean. You know I don't like that kind of talk."

"I said they're not all human," Becky repeated. She reached into the box and pulled out a tooth as long as my finger. It had a silver wire twisted around it that held a tag. "This is from a Kodiak bear. Besides, all the *homo sapiens* examples are from celebrities." She pulled out another tooth that might have been a molar. "This is Justin Bieber's. If I ever meet him, I'm going to get him to sign the tag. It'll be worth millions."

"Oh, and just how do you know that's really his? And what do you think Justin Bieber's going to do when some frizzy-haired little girl wanders up to him and asks him to sign one of his teeth?"

Becky glowered at me. She shoved a curl away from her face. "I do not have frizzy hair! It's flyaway. Isn't that right, Mom?"

Mom looked up from her book again. "Yes, dear. Dean, be nicer to your sister."

Mom gave me a stern look and then nodded to the floor where half of Becky's collection lay scattered. The place looked like a dentist's office had exploded. Becky narrowed her eyes and stared at me. I groaned and crouched to pick up the disgusting bits and muttered, "I didn't mean to knock them out of the box." Dropping the last tooth in, I wiped my hands on my jeans. "Do you have to get shots for handling this kind of germy junk?"

Becky dangled a triangular tooth that even I knew belonged to a shark. "My collections are unique. One of a kind."

I leaned closer. "And they'll all be on display someday. They'll be Exhibit A in your trial after they find the bodies you buried."

"I heard that, Dean," Dad said. "I think you could learn something from Becky. Hobbies like collecting items are terrific outlets for stress. You could use an outlet for stress."

Becky stuck her tongue out at me. But she didn't say anything. She knew about my visions—sort of. She also knew I'd saved her life once. But she didn't know about the secret society.

A jet engine roared overhead, and Becky pointed at the ceiling. "That's where I'm going today."

"Somewhere far away in a plane?" I asked. I gave her my nicest smile.

Becky turned away from me and looked at Mom. "Jasmine and I are going to the fairgrounds. Some of the pilots are signing autographs today."

Abbotsford has one real claim to fame—the annual air show. The idea of bumping into thousands of people at the showgrounds made me shiver and want to hide under my bed. Touch set off my visions, and I didn't want to know how many of those strangers might need me to save them. I remembered the first time that had happened after being trampled during the Gadget Emporium sale. I was bumped, shoved, and generally knocked around by who knows how many people. Those first few visions were forever seared into my mind. I had no idea who the people were, which made the visions even more freakish; the only thing I knew about them was they'd died.

I knew what was coming. Mom or Dad would ask me to go with Becky and keep an eye on her. I could feel it.

Before they could say anything, I said, "I'm meeting Lisa and Colin."

Dad stared at me. "Oh? What are you three up to today?"

"We're going into the city to hang out. Maybe the mall. Air-conditioning, you know"

"Bor-ing," Becky muttered.

I grabbed my windbreaker from the closet, opened the door, and glanced out. Lisa and Colin were walking down the street. Perfect timing.

"Keep your phone handy," Dad called out. "Just in case we need to reach you, or if you ... need ... anything."

Like a new brain, maybe. He didn't say the words, but I could just about hear him thinking it.

I waved and rushed out, catching up to them just about a block from my house. I'd barely had a chance to say hi when tires screeched up ahead. A black Honda Accord roared off a side street and onto ours. Lisa gripped my arm with one hand and Colin's with her other. I instantly had a flashback to the black BMW I'd jumped in front of to save my sister and cringed away from that painful memory of weeks and weeks in casts. The engine roar vibrated across my skin as the car raced toward us.

The three of us stood there as the vehicle squealed to a stop next to us, the tires smoking.

Morning sunlight glinted off the windshield and

made it impossible to see the driver, but the passenger-side window rolled down. Archer Astley—our Society contact—leaned over, his sandy hair ruffled, a worried look tugging on his narrow, lean face. "Get in. We don't have a lot of time."

"What's going on?" Lisa asked. She blinked, and under her summer tan, her face turned pale. "Is someone going to die?"

A blank look descended over Archer's face. My stomach knotted.

Voice urgent, Archer said, "I'll explain everything on the way."

CHAPTER 3

We scrambled into Archer's car, Colin first, then Lisa, and finally me. Colin and Lisa took the back, leaving me to ride shotgun. Archer tore off before we could get our seat belts fastened.

"Something's wrong, right?" I asked, struggling to get the buckle to click. "What is it?"

"One guess," he said. The car squealed around a corner, and I wondered how Archer could drive like this without getting tickets. Or hitting someone.

"Someone's going to die," Lisa said.

"Yeah, us," Colin muttered. I glanced back and saw him hanging on to the strap of his seat belt.

Archer smiled and glanced into his rearview mirror. "Actually, Lisa, someone is scheduled to have an accident. But the dying part shouldn't happen. The four of us are going to see if we can help fix things."

The knot in my stomach tightened. I hated this part, knowing someone's life depended on me—on us. "I haven't had any visions. How long do we have?"

"Two hours. But this case is a little unusual. One of

our members in Japan had this vision."

From the backseat, Colin leaned forward. "We're obviously not going to Japan. I don't even have my passport, and I promised my mom I wouldn't be back too late."

Archer laughed.

"He's right, though," Lisa said. "What's this about?"

"And why only two hours?" I said. "What went wrong? The visions come twenty-four hours in advance of someone's possible death. Why didn't someone get to this person sooner?" I knew how hard it was to keep track of people you were meant to save. I'd have understood if Archer said he'd lost them. In fact, it would be nice to hear that someone else had the same problems I'd had.

Archer accelerated past a UPS truck and jerked the wheel toward a highway on-ramp. "In general, CS members cover their own territory. We're handling this one because the Society member who had the vision is in Japan, and the person they had a vision of came here for the air show. There's another local team meeting us to help. So this is also a chance for you three to see firsthand how the CS functions. We still have to hurry. These last-minute saves are always a bit tricky, but we do have these." Leaning forward, Archer pulled out a plastic bag with phones. He gave one to me and tossed the other two in back.

The phone lay cool and slick in my hand, wrapped in a purple protective case. I flipped it over and tapped the screen. The front side lit, and the initials DC glowed at me in bright yellow. I shivered. It seemed like a chill fog had wrapped around me. *DC*. Obviously they were my initials. But I couldn't help but think about the letters Mr. Vidmar— the man who'd given me the gift of visions—had written on the stopwatch he'd used to count down the end of my life. It reminded me that I was alive because of someone in the Society, and if I could be saved, so could everyone else. I tapped the stopwatch app and saw the numbers count down. Did I really want a phone that kept me better connected to people who were going to die?

From the backseat, I heard Lisa say, "These are incredible. They're ours? Really?"

Archer sped up a little faster. "You can access the CS database as needed. You'll receive mission alerts, video messages, and—" Archer sighed as he heard Colin's phone beeping and squawking. "And yes, I believe they have the latest version of Angry Birds, as well as some actual helpful apps."

Colin quickly turned off the game. "Sorry."

Glancing at me, Archer reached over and tapped a protruding part on my phone. "That piece at the top edge. Slide it out. It's a wireless earbud." I pulled it out and pressed it into my ear. I glanced back to see Colin and Lisa doing the same thing. Archer pointed to my phone again. "Now tap the globe application."

I tapped the image of the spinning world. The phone chimed, and a list of names appeared. White highlighted the top name.

YAMADA.

"Tap the first name ... and pay attention. You'll see the call from one of the Japanese districts."

Fingers cold and palms sweating, I pressed the name. The screen flashed. A video started, showing some kind of conference room with people sitting around a large wooden table. I recognized Archer. He looked up when a woman wearing jeans and a tank top, with short, dark hair, entered the room.

"We have a priority message from Japan." The woman turned and pointed something at the large screen over her shoulder. The image I was watching flashed, and the conference room vanished, replaced by a split-screen image of the dark-haired woman on one side and a Japanese man in a business suit and glasses on the other. He gave a small bow. "Good to see you again, Sarah Pickett."

Sarah gave a small bow too. "Mr. Hayashi. It's been too long."

"We have a most urgent matter," Mr. Hayashi said. He held up a blurred photo of what looked like a middle-aged

Japanese woman. I could see only short, dark hair and a blurry face. "Mrs. Noriko Yamada from Yokkaichi, central Japan. It took us a very long time to track her down, and this is our only photo. Can you reach her in time? We know she is staying at Harrison Hot Springs. The vision showed her wet, wearing a bathing suit and a ..." He glanced off screen and said something in Japanese that sounded like *yogi boshi.*

Another voice answered him, saying, "*Suimu hatto.*"

"Ah, yes, a swim hat," Mr. Hayashi said. "With a floral print. Very distinctive."

"Send us everything you have," Sarah Pickett said.

Hayashi nodded. The screen flashed again, back to the conference room. The woman named Sarah looked at Archer. He stood up and said, "I want to pick up Dean's team for this. They're not far from those hot springs."

Dean's team? Was it my team? Did that make me a leader or something? Just who was this Sarah that she could order Archer around? And what did Lisa and Colin think about being on *my* team? I didn't want to turn around to see if they were happy about this or not.

On the screen, a man in his early twenties with shaggy brown hair stepped forward so he stood close to Sarah. "We'll be primary, and Archer can be the secondary."

"I don't think that's necessary," Archer said. He didn't sound or look too happy when he stared at the other guy.

Sarah shook her head. "Nathan's right. We need to move fast. Now go."

The video cut out, and the display flashed back to the list of names.

From the backseat, Lisa asked, "So that's how it works? You have divisions of the CS all over the world and you contact each other for help?"

"Pretty much," Archer said. "We call them zones and districts. You three are part of the Lower Mainland district. Sarah is our zone leader. But your team reports first to me—I'm your mentor."

"Our team," Colin said. He sounded smug about it.

"*Dean's* team," Lisa said, nudging my shoulder from behind.

I glanced back, and Colin threw me a sloppy salute. "What will you have me do, *mon capitaine*?"

"Oh, give me a break," I muttered.

The car swerved as Archer took the next exit off the highway. A sign pointed left to Harrison Hot Springs. "There's never been a better time to be part of the CS. The tech, and the prevalence of social media, makes it possible to identify and track down the people in our visions like never before. Identification is always the first step to saving someone who shouldn't have to die."

"And you record all your meetings?" Colin asked.

Archer nodded. "There are cameras in all the

conference rooms. Meetings there are always recorded." He tapped my phone. "And speaking of recordings, whenever circumstances permit, carry your phone with the camera lens clear. There's a video app that you can set to record continuously. It's all uploaded to our database. If you ever have a vision of someone you don't recognize, you can use the composite application to create a rough image. We use that to scan our database first before expanding the search online. Once we have an ID from any image, we can track down schedules, credit card transactions, and just about anything else."

"That sounds ... intrusive," Lisa said.

Colin gave a snort. "Give me a break. What's intrusive about tracking someone down to save their life?"

I agreed with Colin and activated the application on my phone. I wasn't sure how often I'd have the phone out of my pocket, but when I did, I wanted it recording. The more help, the better, as far as I was concerned.

"Lisa has a point," Archer said. "The choice is always up to the individual CS member about how to approach an identification. There have been instances where members have misused resources. I was part of a district in Texas where one member faked a vision about a girl just to acquire her name, address, and personal details so he could ask her out."

Colin laughed. "Maybe Dean could do that with Rylee."

Before Archer could ask who Rylee was, I said, "It's too bad the Japan office didn't have better information, so maybe we could avoid a rush right now."

"Oh, they have just as much tech as we do. The problem here was that the member who had the vision knew Mrs. Yamada and tried to track her down on her own. She waited too long to ask for help. By the time she reported the vision, Mrs. Yamada was already on a plane to Abbotsford." Archer glanced at me. "It's a good lesson for us all. We work better in teams."

I sank down in my seat. I did feel sometimes like it was all on me. I had the visions, so it was up to me to figure out who might die. However, I couldn't always figure out what the visions meant. And sometimes they were just too weird. I wondered if Archer was going to say anything else, but he turned the car down a road and in to an area that looked like a type of resort. I saw a lake, a lot of grass and flowers, and little shops and restaurants wherever I looked. He turned down another street and we approached a big hotel that looked like it had been constructed of wood and stone. Archer pulled up right in front, got out, and tossed the keys to the valet. I scrambled out after him, and Lisa and Colin climbed out of the car too.

Glancing at the crowds coming and going—a lot of them Japanese—I turned to Archer and asked, "Where do we start?"

CHAPTER 4

Archer glanced around. He looked as worried as I felt. This place was big—really big. "The woman in the vision was wet. That means she probably has an accident in a pool."

"Or the lake," Colin said, glancing around.

Lisa pushed strands of hair from her face. "Or the hot springs, even. What about the other team? That younger guy in the video. Are they here? Is he the leader of another team?"

"Nathan?" Archer frowned and shook his head. "He's an apprentice. A lot like you guys, only ... well, I won't go into that right now. We're actually ahead of them. I've already texted them to cover the lake and come in from that side of the resort. Whoever finds Mrs. Yamada first will call for backup." He hesitated for a second and then added, "And ... well, Nathan ... Dean, you want to be careful there. Arsney Vidmar, the man you received your gift from, was Nathan's mentor. I'm pretty sure Nathan figured he'd get Vidmar's gift. Obviously he didn't and he really wishes someone would give it to him already."

"Ouch," Colin said. "That would suck getting cheated

like that."

"I'm sure he'd agree with you. But let's focus on keeping Mrs. Yamada out of the pools until after we know she's safe. That would be ideal. Any of you know Japanese?"

I turned around to stare at Colin just as Lisa nudged him. He glanced from her to me and held up a hand, shaking his head. "It was one semester. I hardly remember any of it except maybe how to ask for a check or the bathroom."

I stared at him. "What about when you made me watch all those anime movies? You even translated one."

He lifted a shoulder and offered a lopsided smile. "Well ... I might have been making some educated guesses."

"Making it up," Lisa muttered.

Archer started for the lobby, and we trailed after him. "Let's hope you remember something when it matters."

"Yeah," Colin said, lagging behind us. "Maybe."

We stepped into the lobby, and I glanced around. It was still pretty early but the place was full of people. I heard them speaking all kinds of languages, too. A lot of folks travel a long way to see the air show, but I had no idea so many came from other countries or that Harrison Hot Springs was such a tourist destination. I shivered and tried to avoid touching anyone. I didn't really like the idea of being connected to someone from another country— someone I might have a vision of and be a million miles away from. Just dealing with this vision, a vision from someone else, someone I'd never met, was enough to knot my shoulders and have me sweating. Then again, I couldn't stop wondering about this Nathan guy, too.

Mr. Vidmar hadn't asked me if I wanted the gift, the one Nathan was supposed to get. Vidmar was a mess at the time—beaten, almost unconscious. I remembered him coughing blood on me and then the touch. I remember that. He grabbed me and said, "Glimpse." That touch and that word had changed my life. Still, there were times when I wasn't entirely sure if having these visions was a gift or a curse.

Archer pointed to a sign that had arrows directing visitors to restrooms, a café, and pools. *Pools?* As in more than one? I gave a soft groan. "You three go to the pools in case she's already there. I'm going to try and contact her room from the front desk and see if I can intercept her before she even gets outside. And, Dean, if you're not sure who Mrs. Yamada is, touch anyone who you think might be her. If one of us can connect with her, we'll know if we're close enough to do something when the time comes."

Touch everyone? Yeah, because that wouldn't be at all awkward or inappropriate. Plus it kind of wrecked my plan *not* to connect myself with a bunch of foreign strangers. I tried not to overthink what I had to do. It was for the greater good.

Archer headed to the front desk, and I pulled out my phone to look at the photo again. Lisa leaned over my shoulder. "It really is blurry enough to be almost anyone," she said.

Colin glanced at her. "Yeah, but how hard is it going to be to find an old Japanese lady wearing a flower-printed swim cap? Who even wears those things anyway?"

I nodded and swallowed. My mouth had gone dry. When you have the gift, and you've touched someone who is about to die when they're not supposed to, you get a vision. The world goes gray, and you sort of see how they'll die or, at least, how they'll look the moment before they die. You also get a second vision—a warning really, and only if you're close enough to the person to actually do something. The second vision comes moments before the death, and it's not as freaky. It's just colorblindness—you don't actually see the person. Still, that's two chances. Archer had said to touch anyone to find her—and hopefully touch the right person in the process. I had to anyway, so I'd know if we'd managed to save her from dying. Nonetheless, the thought of possibly having to touch a lot of old Japanese ladies—and there seemed to be more than a few in the lobby—left me feeling like a creep. This wasn't going to be fun. A lot of them would probably slug me.

Colin started walking. "C'mon. I know the way to the pool."

Outside, I had to shade my eyes with my hand. The sun seemed way brighter after the cool, dark hotel lobby. Light glinted off water. A breeze rustled some trees. Blinking, I glanced around.

The place had several pools, all built to look naturally carved into the rocks, with trees and grass planted around them and brick paths that wound through the grounds. The pools were obviously fed by the hot springs, as steam rose off into the air and swirled into shapes. Music played in the background—something cheesy, generic, and bland. At least two dozen Japanese-looking women sat near one of the pools on chairs, wearing white robes. More women and men strolled around, and I couldn't even begin to say if they were locals or from out of town. Some had towels hung over their shoulders. Others walked purpose-fully, seemingly heading somewhere down the curving paths. I couldn't tell anyone's age. All the ladies seemed to be old enough to be at least my mom's age. Any one of them could've been Mrs. Yamada as far as I could tell—except for the blond or the gray-haired ladies. At least half of the older women carried a swim cap with flowers dangling from their fingers. Blue flowers, pink flowers, bright purple flowers.

I smacked my forehead with my palm. "You have to be kidding me. It's some kind of convention for old Japanese ladies."

Lisa bit her lower lip and shoved me forward. "You have to touch them. All of them. We'll start asking for names."

I turned on her. "I can't do that. I'll ... I'll get arrested."

Cupping his hands around his mouth, Colin shouted, "Yamada-san!"

I cringed. Several women turned toward us, probably to see what crazy kid had screamed. Lisa nudged Colin and me again. She nodded to her right where a woman with a name tag and what looked like a hotel uniform of tan pants and a tan shirt stood in a booth with stacks of towels in front of her.

I went over to the towel lady. "Excuse me, do you know a Mrs. Yamada?"

She stared at me and asked, "Just where are your parents?"

Mouth pressed tight, I turned away. We didn't have time for delays.

Colin stepped up to one of the Japanese women who had turned when he'd called out and stuttered, "Um ... Yamada-san? *Dare ga* ... um?"

The women giggled and said, "Which Mrs. Yamada do you want? I know of at least ten of us staying here."

Colin's face reddened. "Ten Yamadas?"

She giggled again, and so did the other ladies.

"What's the joke?" I asked.

"Yamada. Very common name in Japan. It is like asking for a Smith here in America. You have a lot of Mrs. Smiths; we have many Mrs. Yamadas."

"Oh great. That's terrific," Colin muttered. He scratched his head. "Noriko." He looked at Lisa. "That was her first name, wasn't it?"

Lisa nodded. "Yeah, Noriko. I'm sure that was it."

I thought so too and glanced at the ladies.

"Ah, Noriko-chan," one of the ladies said. She glanced around. "I did see her earlier." She said something in Japanese to the other ladies and they looked around and shook their heads. "If we see her, we'll say you're looking for her."

Lisa grabbed my arm and dragged me a step away. "We don't have time for this. You have to start touching people."

Sweat popped on my upper lip, and not just from the heat of the sun. My T-shirt stuck to my back, and I groaned. "Okay, okay ..."

We ducked past the group we'd talked to, and followed another group of Asian ladies to an area with tables, chairs, and shaded awnings. I reached out and brushed the hand or arm of every one of them, wincing as

I did. Most of them shot me surprised or startled looks. A couple of them glared at me. I wouldn't even know if I'd touched the right person until the last few moments, but I had to move quick. Colin stayed next to me and kept saying, "*Yamada-san, desu ka?*"

"What are you doing?" I hissed at him.

He leaned closer. "I'm asking, 'Are you Mrs. Yamada?'"

"Are you sure you're not saying my friend is a pervert nutcase?"

He laughed. "No, but when we're done here, I'm going to learn how to say that in a dozen languages so I'm ready the next time we have to do something like this."

Lisa gave a frustrated growl and stopped. "This is taking too long. We've got to split up. I'll check the changing rooms. You two search opposite sides of the pools. Keep looking for swimming caps with flowers."

She took off before I could say anything. Colin glanced at me. I shrugged. I didn't have a better plan. We saw two more pools now, with trees, winding paths, and shaded areas with tables and chairs. None of the pools had many people, but the areas were pretty big and really spread out. I spotted at least half a dozen women wearing flowered bathing caps in the pools, bobbing around and talking in what had to be Japanese. Any of them could be Mrs. Yamada. To touch them, I'd have jump in the water. I wondered how long it would take for security to drag me away if I did that.

"I can't get to everyone!"

Colin took a deep breath and let it out in a single burst. "Okay, if we can't figure out which one is Mrs. Yamada, we need to just get everyone out of the water, right?"

"Like a fire alarm?" I squinted at Colin. Had he lost his mind?

Colin shook his head and gave me a *you are too dumb* look. "We're outside with water all around. Anyone in a pool is safe from a fire."

"Right. Just double-checking ... and stressing." I held up my phone and showed him the time. "It's way over an hour since Archer told us we only had two hours."

Colin nodded and pulled a chocolate bar from his pocket. "Lucky for you, I have a plan."

"Oh, no. Not like summer camp."

"Oh, yeah. Just like." He tore off the wrapper, broke the gooey, melting bar into chunks and started tossing them into the pools. He was able to get pieces into three of them.

"C'mon, that's not going to work," I said, bumping his arm with my elbow.

Colin smirked. In seconds, the warm water had swirled the chocolate into brown smears. I had to admit, it looked real.

"Look, Mommy," a little boy called out. "Poop!"

The kid's high voice cut through all the other chatter and lifted up over the music playing in the background. I'm pretty sure it was the kid's mom who screamed first. That got everyone moving. A girl in the other pool yelled and jumped out of the water with a chocolaty streak down her arm. She kept shrieking like she'd been bitten by a snake.

From behind, I heard Lisa say, "Colin, did you do that?"

"Mission accomplished," Colin said, dusting his hands. "No one's going to drown today."

Lisa propped a fist on one hip. "According to the vision, she's wet and wearing a swimming cap. For all we know, she slips in this panic you started, falls, and that kills her!"

Pulling in a breath, I pushed into the crowd gathering to stare into the stained pools. I bumped into at least half the people, muttering, "Sorry. Sorry." I held my breath at every touch, but nothing happened. Everyone seemed so interested in the pools that no one even looked at me. I knew we were close to running out of time, even though I didn't look at the clock on my phone. I didn't want to see if we were too late already. I kept hoping the other team with that Nathan guy had already found Mrs. Yamada. But it wasn't good that Archer hadn't joined us yet. He was probably having as much trouble as we were.

Two guys who looked Asian headed toward me from the far side of the pool. I kept brushing against anyone and everyone. I didn't even care now if it was a woman or a man or a kid or an old person. Panic tightened my chest and closed my throat. I forced out rasping breaths, and my heart hammered away against my ribs.

Just as the two guys walked past, I asked, "Excuse me. Do you guys speak English? Do you know a Mrs. Yamada? Noriko Yamada?"

One of the guys stared at me like I had some of Colin's chocolate smeared on my face. "Yeah, I speak English." He didn't have an accent. My cheeks burned for being such an idiot to think they might speak only Japanese. Then he added, "Mrs. Yamada's over there." He gestured over his shoulder, and he and his friend pushed past me.

I followed where he'd pointed and spotted a young Asian woman sitting on a lounge chair. The bikini and the rest of her didn't look anything like the blurred image I had of a woman twice her age. But an older woman sat up from a chair behind the younger woman. I headed for her. The middle-aged woman walked to the edge of the pool. I cut around another pool and pushed past more people gawking at the brown, swirling streaks. The older woman stood beside a pool and pulled on a swim cap with bright yellow and orange flowers.

I could swear a band of energy seemed to snap between me and her. I might have been imagining it— maybe I wanted so badly for her to be the right person that

I'd felt something that wasn't there. I shook my head. I couldn't overthink this. It had to be her. Heart pounding like I'd just run ten miles, I knew I had only a couple minutes. She stood at the edge of the pool. I imagined her diving in and smashing her head on the bottom. Or slipping and splattering her brains on the rocks around the pool.

"Mrs. Yamada. Wait!" I ran the rest of the way around the pool, waving my hands, not caring if I looked like a maniac.

The woman stepped away from the pool and ducked behind the younger one who had gotten to her feet and stood between me and the older lady, holding out one hand to stop me. "Who are you?" she demanded.

"Oh ... I ... you speak English, too." Okay, did everyone in Japan speak English as well as Japanese? "Sorry, it's just I'm looking for a Mrs. Yamada from Japan. Mrs. Noriko Yamada."

The young woman narrowed her eyes, but her shoulders relaxed. "You don't look like you're from the hotel."

"Please, lady. It's really important."

I could see her thinking about it, but she glanced at the older woman. They spoke to each other in Japanese, and the young woman turned back to me. "This is Mrs. Noriko Yamada. She's my aunt. She wants to know why you're looking for her."

"Just don't go near the water." I glanced at my phone. "At least not for the next five minutes or so. It's ... there's something wrong with the pools." I gestured to the other pools that had emptied out. People were still standing around and staring at the water. Tapping my phone screen, I texted Archer, letting him know I'd found Mrs. Yamada. He texted back that he'd track me by my phone's GPS and would meet me. **STAY PUT**, the text ordered.

Letting out a breath, I looked up and smiled at the two women, but the older woman had gone really gray. Oh, no—not a vision. I blinked. She was still gray, and it was as if a ripple spread outward from the woman pulling all the color out of the scene around me.

It was happening. Now!

"Are you feeling okay?" I asked her.

The woman glanced at me and asked, her voice soft and strained, "*Nani?*"

The younger woman looked at her aunt. "*Obasan. Daijobu.*" She turned to me and folded her arms. "Just what is going on here? You know what, never mind." She grabbed a towel from her chair and yelled, "Security!"

The color was fully gone. The pool had gone from sparkling blue to a swirling gray. "It's still happening," I muttered. I whirled, hoping to spot whatever danger was headed for the older woman. I saw only the empty pools and people in the distance, standing around in small groups, looking down at the chocolate-bar scene Colin had created. Suddenly, it clicked. My gut churned, and I nearly threw up.

I turned to stare at the older woman. "I didn't touch you yet."

Both of them retreated, and the younger woman held out her towel in front of her. "If you try to touch either one of us—"

"No. No. That means it can't be her. It's still the wrong Yamada. The wrong Yamada." I whirled around.

I was experiencing what would have been my second warning if I'd been the one to have a vision of Yamada in the first place. It was the colorblindness—so I must've touched the right Mrs. Yamada at some point since we arrived at the hot springs. I tried to remember all the people I'd seen in the hotel. Who had I touched? I'd rushed past lots of people, bumping into at least a dozen or more. But where was she now?

I wouldn't have had this warning if I hadn't been close enough to do something. That was the rule, wasn't it? I had to get a better view.

Turning, I stared up at the rocks around this pool. They created the highest point out here. It would have to do. I climbed up on them, my hands burning as I scraped my skin. The world spun and swirled into gray. Dizzy, I clung to the top rock and turned. I stared out at the pools. I could see three of them with trees and paths dotted between, all of them ashen and hazy. The world seemed to slow, as if even time had started to crawl. One pool empty. Another also empty. Another ... and that's when I saw her.

Black edged my vision, but I saw the woman in the water, right beside the edge of a small pool tucked away from the others. Thick palms and other plants hid the edges of it. I could see it only because I clung to the high outcropping of rocks.

I shouted and pointed to Colin and Lisa. I half fell and half climbed down the rocks, jumping the last couple of feet. I hit the pavement hard, and pain jolted up into my knees. Staggering, I ran for the small pool. Colin got there just before me. He jumped into the water. I heard Lisa yelling for help, for security, for a lifeguard. With all the strength I had, I jumped in too.

The water felt like a bath.

I pushed off the bottom, against the dragging weight of my clothes, knowing what I'd see when I surfaced. I knew because of Colin's face. I knew because the woman floated, her face down in the water. I knew because the color bled back into the world around me. The second vision ended only after the window to save someone ends. When that person is saved ... or when it's too late.

CHAPTER 5

I stood beside the pool with a towel wrapped around me, unable to move. Everything seemed like a movie. It all seemed like something that wasn't really happening. Colin had pulled the woman out of the water. I think I helped, but I couldn't remember doing anything. He'd started CPR, pressing on her chest and giving her rescue breaths. Lisa got there with help from the hotel. Sirens screamed. My clothes clung to me, wet and cold. Someone had put a towel over my shoulders. I sneezed.

Archer arrived at some point. He looked around, his expression seeming calm. But when his stare met mine, I saw the sadness in his eyes. I turned away.

It didn't matter what anyone did. I knew it. I could tell by the way Archer had looked at me that he knew it, too. Mrs. Yamada was dead. I'd seen this same thing happen when my neighbor had died. I'd had a chance. The moment was there, and all I had to do was act at the right time. I'd been too late ... once again.

Shivering, I wanted to yell that I had been with Mrs. Yamada. I thought I'd found the right one. Glancing over, I saw she seemed fine. She was watching the scene, one hand pressed to her mouth, her eyes bright with tears. We'd missed the person we'd come here to save.

I'd missed her.

A hand grabbed my shoulder. I turned to see Colin watching me, his face pale and his hair plastered to his head. "C'mon," he said in an urgent whisper.

I glanced at the dead woman. People in uniforms had taken over the CPR from Colin. They put her on a stretcher. Wires ran from a machine in a red bag to sticky pads attached to her chest—a defibrillator that jump-starts hearts.

"Now!" Colin said, hissing the word into my ear.

He was right. We had to go before someone started asking us questions. The CS had to stay a secret. I dropped the towel, and Colin pulled me back the way I'd come, away from the dead woman and the people still trying to save her. Lisa fell into step with us. We followed Archer to a gate in a back fence that led around to the parking lot. We trudged to his car and stood outside of it as he jogged the dozen meters to the valet to get his keys. Even in the hot sun, I kept shivering.

Colin squeezed water out of his hair. He looked at me. "What the heck happened? I got your text to Archer, too, Dean. You said you had her. You said you were with Mrs. Yamada."

"I was." I shook my head. "I was with her."

"You were with *a* Mrs. Noriko Yamada," Archer said as he jogged back and unlocked the doors. "Not *the* Mrs. Noriko Yamada. I'd only just discovered there was more than one woman at this one hotel with that name after you texted me."

"But we got her in time, right?" Colin asked. "I am sure I was in the water before the time ran out."

"Is that true?" Lisa asked, her tone practically begging for it to be true. Her eyes seemed really big, and red rimmed the edges. "Is she going to make it?"

Archer stared at me. "You connected with her somehow, didn't you? You touched her."

I nodded and hunched one shoulder. "I must've bumped into her in the lobby or ... or at some point."

Archer blew out a breath and scrubbed a hand through his hair. "So, you experienced the second warning? You lost color vision just before it happened?"

"Hey, Dean's the reason I even saw her," Colin said. "You pointed her out."

I took a breath. Held it. Let it out. I had to say something, but I just wanted to crawl into the car and get away from here. "I didn't realize what was happening until it was too late."

Lisa hugged her arms around herself. "She's going to make it. I know it. The paramedics got here right away.

They had stuff to save her." As if to back up her words, an ambulance screamed past us, leaving the hotel parking lot. "See. If she was dead, they wouldn't bother with sirens. They wouldn't be speeding."

Archer turned and stared at the ambulance. I think he was thinking the same thing I was. Sure, they're speeding. Sure, they're still trying to save her. They'd go on trying, but it wouldn't do any good. I'm not sure how long we stood there, but my T-shirt dried. My jeans still clung to my legs, wet and stiff. I reeked of chlorine. So did Colin. No one said anything. Lisa turned away, sniffing, her head bowed. I heard Colin swear under his breath, using words that my mom would have told him he shouldn't know.

It was times like this that I actually wished we could tell Dr. Mickelsen about the visions. The thought of therapy reminded me we were supposed to go to the museum at some point. None of that really seemed to matter right now.

"Let's go," Archer said at last. He opened the driver's door, but a battered yellow Volkswagen pulled up across the front of Archer's Honda.

Archer closed his door and stepped forward.

Two men got out of the Volkswagen. The younger guy with the long hair, the black polo shirt, and the expensive designer jeans looked like Nathan, the guy we'd seen in the video. He pulled off his sunglasses and glanced at us, his eyes narrowed. The other guy, with short, gray hair, looked way older than Archer. Sunlight glared off his button-down white shirt. The older guy tugged at his chino pants like he had the belt too tight. "We heard the sirens. What happened?"

Archer didn't say anything, but the look on his face must've said, "She's dead." The older man locked his fingers behind his head and turned away, muttering angrily.

The younger guy, Nathan, walked over to us and stopped right in front of me. "You must be Dean."

He said it like he was measuring up my name, or maybe me.

I glanced at Colin and then Lisa. They both stared at Nathan, Colin looking wary and Lisa rubbing at her red eyes. I looked at Nathan again but I couldn't really tell what he was thinking. Did he think I had stolen something that should have been his? He had a narrow face and pale blue, close-set eyes. He smiled at me. He held out his hand. "I'm Nathan Headwell. I hoped we'd all be meeting up to celebrate a save."

Reluctantly, I shook his hand.

He gestured to the man he'd arrived with. "This is Hank Fallston."

Hank whirled back around, taking a few steps until he stood in front of Archer. "We all saw Dean's text to you. He said he had Mrs. Yamada. What happened?"

Archer shook his head and said, his voice dropping low, "Hank, we can do this during debriefing."

I stepped forward. "I had the wrong Yamada. I'm sorry." My voice sounded weak and that bothered me. *Weak* wasn't the impression I wanted to give to these people.

Everyone stared at me. Nathan folded his arms and seemed to be studying me again, his head tipped to one side. Hank narrowed his eyes, and I could see the pulse jumping in his hard jaw.

Archer glanced at me. "Dean, you don't need to apologize. And you don't need to talk about this right now, either. It happens. It's regrettable, but I told you before that these kinds of missions can be tough. This one was especially challenging."

"You don't call everyone else off unless you are one hundred percent certain you have the right person." Hank slashed the air with his hand. "This is why kids have no place in the CS!"

Archer stepped between me and Hank. "Dean has done a good job so far. He's still learning. There were two women here who had the exact same name. How could he know that? Dean did good."

"Good?" Hank gave a short, barking laugh. "According to you? Archer, that kid has broken laws. He doesn't seem to even know what a rule is for!"

"He and his friends have saved lives."

"And trashed a museum. They're irresponsible. They're more interested in becoming thieves and hoodlums than saving lives. You want to mentor kids? You think they should be members of the CS? You want to bend rules until they break? That kind of approach is going to cost us lives, lives we could have saved. Today only proves my point!"

"Today could have happened to anyone in the CS."

Hank leaned forward, his hand lifted threateningly. But he glanced at us and motioned Archer to go with him. He moved to the far side of the yellow Volkswagen where we couldn't hear what they might say. Archer glanced at us, stuffed his hands into his pockets, and followed Hank. I watched as Hank turned red while he ranted at Archer, his face tight and his words just an angry muttering carried away by the breeze.

I glanced at Nathan, who leaned against Archer's car, his legs crossed at the ankles. "Why does Archer take that from Hank?"

Nathan lifted his eyebrows. "Hank's one of the most senior members of the CS. Archer better listen to him. Hank is Archer's boss's boss. But Archer is right, guys. This happens. When I was mentoring with Vidmar, he used to get upset over every fail. Maybe not as upset as Hank, but pretty close. I'm sure you'll learn how to better use your gift as you go along. It's tough being in the CS."

"We heard you were Vidmar's apprentice," Colin said. He folded his arms as though waiting for Nathan to say something.

In a voice barely over a whisper, Lisa said, "I'm sorry he died."

Nathan flashed her a warm smile. "Thanks. That's kind of you. But Vidmar knew his days were numbered. He was getting tired. Getting sloppy."

I remembered seeing Vidmar's hospital record when we'd visited him. It was as thick as a textbook and I still remembered how the notations seemed to indicate the doctors thought Vidmar was mentally unstable and possibly suicidal. They'd had it wrong, of course. It appeared that way because Vidmar had put himself in dangerous situations to save lives. But I wondered if maybe Nathan wasn't wrong. Maybe there was a psychological toll. There was obviously a physical one.

Nathan turned, and it felt like he was looking right through me. But his mouth edged up in a crooked smile. "Listen, Dean, I don't know what you might expect, or what you've heard." He glimpsed over to Archer and then back at me. "No hard feelings, right? I wasn't there, and I'm glad Vidmar passed his gift to someone. It would have been doubly tragic if it had died with him. I hope you don't think I'm the kind of jerk who expects the world to revolve

around him and I'm going to go all evil-v
because I was cheated out of a gift that
been promised to me."

He made the words really dramatic as ... . them so
the whole idea sounded silly. I wondered how I would feel
if I lost the gift now. Or if I'd been waiting for it for years.

I shrugged. I had no idea what to say to him, so I just
stood there.

The engine of the Volkswagen roared. Nathan
pushed off the hood of Archer's car. "My cue to go. See
you around."

He strolled over to the vehicle and got in. It zoomed
off, leaving us all choking on the fumes. Archer walked to
his car and climbed in, his lips pressed into a thin line. We
all got in, too, slipping back into our same seats and
buckling up.

I thought about when I'd first been contacted by the
CS and how grateful I was to find out that it wouldn't just
be me, Lisa, and Colin trying to deal with my visions. I'd
thought back then that at least people wouldn't die
anymore because I was too inexperienced to know how to
react. My stomach twisted. It seemed that wasn't the case.

Archer started the engine and pulled out of the
parking lot, driving slow now. "You have my apologies for
everything you just witnessed. Hank Fallston doesn't
handle failure well. And he has some old-fashioned views

ɪ how things should be done. If he had his way, we'd ᴊmp all our technology and travel in the old teams we used to have, trying to do everything with just touch. "

"He's not wrong about some things," I said, thinking how he had blamed me for making mistakes.

"He is, Dean." Archer said as a smile came back into his eyes. "How could any of us have known there'd be more than one Mrs. Yamada? And what if you hadn't sent that text message? Do you think everything would have worked out differently?"

I peered down at my drying jeans and rubbed a finger against them. "I don't know. That's the problem, isn't it? How can I not wonder? If I hadn't been so quick to text …" I stared out the car window at the traffic around us.

Colin leaned forward from the backseat. "What if she had been the right Yamada? The lady you found? What if you hadn't sent that text? What if … what if? You get a headache trying to think about all the stuff that could have happened and didn't. We did the best we could. We came so close. That's what hurts."

Keeping his eyes on the road, Archer said, "Dean, if you really wanted to, you could gift your vision away. You can give it once without anything happening to you, but the second time you gift it, it's gone. You'll be free of the visions, of the Society, of everything."

"Dean," Lisa said softly, "you could be free of it. Free

of the visions."

Archer nodded. "Yes, but you have to be careful. This gift in the wrong hands could be a disaster. Someone could use the gift to force people to pay money in order to be saved. It's one reason why the CS works so hard to try and make sure the gift is given to only those who are prepared to receive the gift."

"I wasn't prepared."

"All the more reason why you want to take your time with deciding how to use the gift. Vidmar saw something in you, or he wouldn't have gifted it to you. I don't think he acted just because he was dying. I think you came to his aid, and he knew he could trust you. That needs to be respected. But when people give up the gift, it's usually right away. Right after the first vision. Or it's when they become very old and can't get the job done. Or it's ..." Archer's face twisted like he was thinking about something painful. He shook his head. "The point is it's a very big deal. Getting the gift and giving it. The gift ... it's worse than giving away an arm or a leg. It's more like gifting part of you. It can be a terrible loss that you never get over. You have to be certain what you want."

I blurted the words out. "I'm not giving anything away. At least ... not right now."

Archer smiled and eased back in his car seat. I thought he seemed to like my response. "Then let's have you meet more of the CS."

We stopped for food on the way back to Abbotsford. It was still a bit early for lunch, and I didn't have an ounce of appetite, but Archer insisted and bought everyone a burger, fries, and a soda. I sat with mine in my lap as we drove. When I checked the back, Lisa was sitting with her arms crossed, staring out the window. Colin was tearing into his food, and Archer ate casually as he drove.

"You seemed pretty comfortable in the water, Colin," Archer said, no doubt trying to ease the tension that practically crackled in the car.

Around muffled bites, Colin said, "Two years junior lifeguard. Never thought I'd use it. My dad thought it'd be a fun summer job for me and wanted me to learn the basics."

"For all the good it did," Lisa muttered.

"That's it," Archer said. He tossed his half-eaten burger back into the white bag between us. He looked over at me and then into the rearview mirror at Lisa. "If you don't learn how to handle failure, you're never going to make it in the CS. I know it's hard, and I want to be patient and help, but you're looking at it wrong." He turned his gaze on Colin. "You seem to be handling it better. Why do you think that is?"

I heard Colin drain his Coke. "Uh ... well? I guess it's because I figure it's like this. We're doing the impossible. If

Dean didn't get a vision, that person's dead anyway. Right? Even with a vision, that person's still as good as dead if something doesn't change. We're kind of fixing things that shouldn't happen, but it's impossible to fix everything."

Archer nodded. "That's a good way to look at it."

"It probably helps, too, that I've been watching people die on movie sets since before I was out of diapers. This is a lot like ... well, like a video game reset button. It's a second chance, isn't it?"

Turning in my seat, I stared at him. "No. It's not like that. This isn't *Halo*. And I can't pretend it is."

"Neither can I," Lisa said.

Anger tore into me, burning in my throat. "I hear the screams of the people I see in visions. They're not screams of fear. It's as if they're desperate for someone to save them. They're begging for help. I see it in their eyes. I feel it!" Turning away from Colin, I muttered, "You don't know."

Beside me, Archer said, his voice soft, "I know it. And you're right. That's exactly how it sounds. And, even so, sometimes we fail. People die. But you know what, Dean? If you don't get past taking that risk of failure, you're going to stop trying to succeed. You won't be able to move on. You won't be able to face your next vision. Or the one after that. The bodies will still pile up, and before you know it, you'll be used up and done."

He nodded ahead of us even though there weren't any

other cars in sight. "That's Hank's problem. He has a hard time with failure. And he doesn't think someone as young as you can handle it. If he had his way, the only people with the gift would be battle-hardened soldiers. And that would be a problem because the CS needs different views and unique talents. We need people who can handle the failures as well as the successes and who do not let either of those things interfere with their ability to act."

I nodded, but even though I heard what he was saying, it didn't fill that empty hole inside me. Mrs. Yamada felt too much like Mr. Utlet, my former neighbor who had been shot right in front of me. He'd died because I didn't act. But I'd acted to try and save Mrs. Yamada, and I hadn't made a difference. How did I get past that?

"So now what?" Colin asked, sounding way too cheerful. I knew he was just trying to make everyone feel better.

"I'd like to go home," Lisa said, her voice really small.

"Sorry. You need to debrief. We talk about the mission. We discuss what went wrong and how to learn from it. We debrief successful missions too, so it's something to get used to."

"It sounds like our therapy sessions," Colin said.

Archer smiled. "Uh, probably less touchy-feely."

I heard the rustle of a bag as Colin stole Lisa's fries, and probably her burger. "Oh, the one thing missing from our sessions with Mickelsen is a hug at the end. Maybe we should ask him about more group hugs."

Colin kept going about how great it would be to see Dr. Mickelsen hug Rodney, who we all agreed probably hadn't ever had a hug in his life. He showed how Mickelsen's arms wouldn't reach around Rodney. That pulled a weak laugh from Lisa and even a smile from me.

Archer turned off the highway. I took a pull of my Coke, peered out the windshield, and blinked. My mouth fell open. Gray shafts of light broke through gray clouds that cast gray shadows around us. "The trees are the same color as the street," I muttered.

Colin stopped his joking and asked, "What are you talking about?"

That's when the man appeared on the hood of the car.

CHAPTER 6

I jolted in my seat, spilling my Coke.

But I knew now what was going on.

A vision.

The man who wasn't really on the car crouched low, staring at me with steely gray eyes. In my vision, his dark hair fluttered in a wind that blew it back. It should have blown forward if he really was on the hood of a car. I glanced at his clothing—gray also. Some kind of coverall like mechanics wear, but this looked fancier, like it fit him really well. He had broad shoulders. The patches on the chest and shoulders made it look like some kind of military uniform. I didn't recognize him and tried to spot a name tag, but didn't see one. A small, dark mustache made a line over a wide mouth, with lines in its corners indicating that he probably smiled a lot. I couldn't tell if he was dark-skinned or light—the gray washed out everything. But I knew I'd never forget his sharp eyes or that strong, hawk-like nose.

It felt like a full minute passed while we stared at each other. I knew it was only a few seconds, and he couldn't really see me. I was seeing a death that should never happen. Bit by bit, he began to twist. I hated this part of the vision—the part where I saw how he would die.

His shoulder dropped. One of his legs jerked forward in an impossible way. His arms twisted back. I flinched. But the vision kept going. I couldn't stop it. And I was unable to look away. The vision held me locked in its gray swirls. The man's mouth opened, slowly at first, but soon his lips spread wider than any human mouth should. His uniform burst into flames and fell away, showing burnt skin and charring bone. I was glad I couldn't smell the fire.

The man started burning to death right before my eyes. I choked back a scream while he let out an inhuman noise. A terrible shriek, lost and begging. I shuddered, feeling like an animal made of ice had clamped its teeth around my spine. The man vanished. I closed my eyes tight.

Slumping in my seat, I let out a shaking breath. I could feel everyone's stare hot on my skin. I knew even Archer was shooting me glances while he drove. From the backseat, Lisa touched a hand to my shoulder. "Is it over?"

I nodded, turned around, and opened my eyes, "Yeah, it's—" My words caught in my throat.

Every single time I'd had a vision so far, the world turned back to color again when the vision ended. As I stared at Colin and Lisa, both of them looked entirely gray.

I jerked my head back and looked at Archer. I was about to ask him what was going on when I saw pain twist his face and darken his eyes. He gripped the steering wheel with one hand and stared straight ahead.

I followed his gaze and saw the gray-washed people on the streets. I gasped. "Are they all—?"

Archer said, his voice tight, "How many do you see?"

"At least a dozen," I whispered.

I recognized almost everyone. They were people I'd seen around Abbotsford. However, I was having a really hard time focusing. The people began to twist. Just like the guy on the hood, they burst into flames. The screams hit my ears—too many voices all at once. Agony. Death. I pressed my palms to my ears, but it didn't muffle the sound that ripped through me.

And then it was over. I let my hands drop. My heart thudded, dull and fast. Color melted back into the world around us.

I breathed in.

Breathed out.

I straightened in my seat and stared at my hands and the dashboard, unwilling to look outside. At least I could see color in the car again. "There had to be ... at least a dozen people."

"That's all you saw?" Archer said. "I saw thirty-three."

"That many?" Colin gasped.

Archer pulled to the side and held up his phone. "Pull up the countdown app on your phones. Set your timers, guys. We have twenty-four hours until we have a disaster on our hands. Dean, you saw something else before I did. Tell me about it."

"I didn't recognize him. I don't think ..." Bile came up into my mouth. I swallowed it back, pressing on, and said, "He died like everyone else. Burned."

Lisa gasped.

Archer slipped his phone into a holder on his dash and touched an icon on the screen. A moment later, the woman we'd seen in an earlier video appeared.

"Sarah, I just—"

"We know," she said. She looked pale, but she cleared her throat and straightened. "Everyone here with the gift just had visions. We're making a list, gathering names, and starting the usual checks. Send us the names of anyone you can ID."

Archer frowned, glanced at me, and asked, "Did anyone at CS have two visions? One practically on top of the other?"

Sarah shook her head. "No. Did you?"

"Dean did. But he says he doesn't know the first guy. And the man in Dean's first vision may be key to what happens to everyone else."

Sarah glanced my way, and I realized the video had to

be two-way. She could see me. My cheeks heated. "Sorry our first chat has to be like this, Dean. I still am looking forward to meeting you, Colin, and Lisa. But please think about the man you saw. You had to have touched him at some point if you had a vision of him, but of course, maybe you didn't realize it. Maybe it was a bump that you didn't even notice. It happens. Consider what he was wearing. Do you remember going somewhere where people wore something similar?"

I shook my head. I knew what I knew—and I had never met that man before. I hadn't had the gift that long. I hadn't been connecting with people for years and years the way Archer had. I'd never touched him. I tried to convince myself that I might have bumped into him early on after getting the gift. He might have been one of the people who'd trampled me in the Gadget Emporium all those months ago. But I couldn't shake the feeling that that wasn't the case at all. That I'd never touched him. And if that were true, did that make me some kind of freak? Were my visions morphing into something else? Something worse? I made a conscious effort to pull myself together.

Sarah kept talking. "Just think about it. We'll talk when you get here. Archer, see you in a few." The screen blanked. Archer placed the phone in the center console and gripped the wheel with both hands.

"Guess we're meeting everyone after all," Lisa said.

She let out a long breath.

"I wish I had other clothes." The car seat squeaked as Colin shifted. "Wet jeans make me feel like I peed myself."

Archer snickered at him. "After what we just saw, you're not going to be the only one needing to change when we get there."

Archer pulled into a two-story strip mall and stopped in an angled parking space. Graffiti swept some of the walls with bright colors over chipped plaster and exposed brick. Different colors marked each shop—bright red for a store, yellow for a laundry, and a tired drab white for a place that had gone out of business.

Nudging Colin as we got out of the car, I said, "Not exactly the Bat Cave."

Colin nodded. "Not exactly a place I'd want to call home—or work."

Lisa caught up with us. "Did you really think it would be a secret lair?"

Swiveling to stare at her, Colin asked, "You didn't? I mean, super-secret society, around for centuries, the gift of visions? At the very least, we ought to be underground, right?"

Archer stood beside a door he'd unlocked. "We have funding, but we decided a long time ago to skip the volcanic secret islands. Takes too long to get anywhere," he said with a smile.

He led us through a door and up a narrow stairwell.

Worn wooden stairs creaked under our steps. Thin wood panels peeled off the walls, looking like something from my grandparents' house. Lisa clung to a narrow rail that wobbled under her touch. I kept my hands to myself.

We reached the top floor and looked around. A grubby beige carpet covered a long hallway with doors on either side. Light spilled out from under the doors, some with business names stenciled on them. Archer led us to a blank, black entrance. Not that I really expected a sign. What would it say? *Welcome to the Congregatio de Sacrificio. Please have a seat and a member of our secret society will be with you shortly.*

"Kinda creepy," muttered Colin, taking it all in. He ran a finger down one of the dingy walls and wiped his hand on his jeans.

Archer stopped by the door. "We try to keep operating expenses to a minimum. You never know when you're going to have to walk away from a place on short notice, but there has been talk for some time of moving."

Colin shook his head. "Be hard to get worse. I've seen tent cities with less dirt."

Archer smiled and led us inside.

We stepped into a large open area with more office doors. The place buzzed like a hornet's nest that had been struck with a rock. People hurried out of other offices, talking on phones, and calling out to one another. A woman behind a reception desk just inside the doorway greeted us. "Welcome back to the circus, Archer."

"Thanks, Doris. I'll get my chair and whip and prepare to enter the lion cage. But first you better meet Dean, Lisa, and Colin. Guys, this is Doris. She's our main tech and the person to see if you need any information."

Doris wiggled her fingers at us, her flowered blouse fluttering as she moved. She had her dark hair pulled back in a ponytail, kind of like Lisa, except Doris's hair stayed slicked back. She was pretty with kind of a round face. She looked like the cool aunt who brings you great presents for your birthday instead of showing up with socks. She was also calm. She barely noticed the noise and people around her.

Her phone rang, but instead of answering it, she turned to the three of us. "I'm really sorry about today. I'm waiting for word from the hospital, and as soon as I have it, I'll let you guys know."

Lisa grabbed my arm and dug her fingernails in. "You mean Mrs. Yamada's still alive?"

Doris nodded. "Paramedics had to restart her heart twice. But she made it to the hospital, and doctors were working on her as of a few minutes ago."

Lisa turned to me. "I thought you said —"

"I did." I turned away from Lisa.

She looked to Archer with an almost pleading expression. I knew she wanted him to tell us that we had really saved Mrs. Yamada. I also knew we had missed the time we had to save Mrs. Yamada. The doctors might have her body on all kinds of life support, but when they stopped that, her body wouldn't be able to hang on. I knew she had already left this world.

"Let's not think about it too much, Lisa," Archer said.

"Archer!" I turned and saw Sarah Pickett walking toward us.

Archer nodded to us. "Sarah, meet Dean, Colin, and Lisa."

She stopped before each one of us, taking one hand between both of hers and taking her time in just holding our hands. It was a little weird. But she had a nice smile and seemed glad to see us. "Great to have you three on the team. Sorry we couldn't have a better orientation, but I promise we'll do that just as soon as we get this latest disaster under control."

"Where are we with that?" Archer asked.

"We're pulling in extra teams from all over the district, and even the districts around us." She gestured us forward and spoke as we followed her. "We've identified at least one employee from Abbotsford Airfield, so we're certain whatever is going to happen will be at the air show. It has to be there. We have other issues, though. Dean, you're the only one who had two visions. You've got to identify the man in your first one. His death comes before anyone else's, so he's got to be the key to saving the others. If we save that one man, we might not have to try and save what seems like up to a few hundred people."

CHAPTER 7

"Save the pilot, save hundreds?" I muttered.

Doris set me up in a tiny office with a thin tablet computer. Archer had asked her to show me the image of every pilot and performer at the air show and photos of all the employees as well. My eyes were ready to cross permanently.

"You'll do fine," Doris said. She brought me a cold soda. So, while Sarah and Archer showed Colin and Lisa around the CS, I got to sit and look at image after image. Guys smiling, women waving, mechanics in grainy group shots beside airplanes ... you name it, I saw it.

I kept swiping the screen and getting more and more frustrated. "Where are you?" I asked the mystery man. And what if he wasn't a pilot at the air show? What if he was some guy who just flew a private Leer in from somewhere and would crash into one of the air show planes? I swiped again, saw another face, swiped again, saw another face. I swiped again—and almost knocked over my drink.

I'd found him.

The guy with the strong nose and sharp eyes stared back with a grin full of confidence. I'd been right. He did smile a lot.

I let out a yell. "It's him!"

A half dozen people rushed in, including Archer. Jumping to my feet, I pointed at the screen. "That's him. That's the guy in my vision."

Archer pulled out his phone and tapped a couple of icons. The same image came up on his phone. He held it out to me. "Karl McKnight. I've reported him to Sarah. We need to learn everything about him and his team. Doris?" He turned and almost bumped into her.

She glanced up from her phone. "Already on it. Flight plan, aircraft specs, his mechanics. Shoe size even. I'll pass the info on to the other teams as it comes in."

I pulled out my phone and immediately started seeing information. "McKnight is Australian." I looked at Archer. "This is his first time at the Abbotsford Air Show. When do you think I could have touched him?"

Archer put a hand on my shoulder. "Don't waste time overthinking it. You touched him, or you wouldn't have had the vision. You probably bumped into him at the hotel this morning, in fact. A lot of people are staying at the hot springs. Trust me, this is a good thing. We know when this disaster is going to happen, and we have an idea of who's going to cause it. I think we can safely say McKnight is going to crash at the show. We can fix this."

I shook my head, and asked, "What if I'm having visions without touching someone?"

Frowning, Archer glanced over his shoulder. Everyone else had left the room. He leaned down. "I don't think you should say things like that. Hank isn't the only one around here who questions your being part of the CS."

"You think even the freaks will think I'm a freak?"

"Having the gift doesn't make you a freak, Dean. Now, let's focus on that information Doris sent on McKnight."

I sat down and tried to read all the stuff, but I couldn't stop thinking about McKnight—especially about seeing him without having touched him.

Sure, I'd been to the air show. I'd always loved it. Who wouldn't? Old planes with four wings, modern jets, big bombers from World War II. Pilots flew stunts, flipping upside down and passing each other with what always seemed like only inches between them. Abbotsford turned its fairgrounds into a carnival with food for sale and people hawking T-shirts and hats and model airplanes. Thousands of visitors from all over the world jammed the grandstands. Sweaty, sunburned, lotion-wearing spectators with their folding chairs and screaming kids just waiting to connect with me.

I shuddered.

All those people meant possible connections.

Possible visions. Possible deaths.

Stop being a baby, I told myself. *It's not all on me this time.* I had to start thinking about what Archer had said. And Colin. Anyone I had a vision of was already dead if we didn't do anything. So, it was time to get out there and do something good.

I pushed my fears into the back of my mind, but another voice rose up. *Who are you kidding? You're terrified.* Yeah, I was. I wanted to be like Archer—cool and smiling and able to get things done no matter what. I bet he'd walk straight through a crowd, high-fiving everyone that he passed. Making connections and not worrying about what it might mean down the road.

Colin burst into the room. "You wouldn't believe all the stuff we've seen!"

Lisa came in right behind him and stared wide-eyed at me. "You all right? You look pale."

I shrugged. "That vision was pretty freaky." I changed the topic and told them about finding McKnight.

But then Lisa cleared her throat and said, "Please tell me the CS really can deal with visions like this. I mean ..." She blew out a breath and muttered, "This is so bad. So many people."

It was easier for me to act like Archer for Lisa. "Archer's already got it under control. You heard him mention other zones and districts." I told them how CS teams from all over were headed here. Lisa's shoulders eased a bit, and Colin's eyes got bigger.

"Boy, when they said we'd meet a few people from the CS, I was thinking, like, about five. Seems like we get to meet everyone all at once."

I thought about saying something about McKnight—how I was sure I had never even seen this guy before today—but Archer was right about that too. We needed to focus on saving a whole lot of people from a crash that was now due to happen—I checked my countdown—in twenty-one and a half hours.

A text popped up on my phone from Archer.

MEETING IN THE WAR ROOM.

Lisa's phone beeped, and then Colin's played the opening music of *Star Wars*. "You already changed your alerts and ring tones?" I asked.

He lifted a brow. "I had to do something during the boring parts of the tour. Where do you think the war room is?"

"Follow the crowd," Lisa said, already heading for the door.

We trailed after Lisa and three other people. We walked into a room I recognized from the video we'd seen in the car. A stab of guilt hit me again for not helping Mrs. Yamada—the *right* one—but I pushed it down. We had a lot of other people who needed us now. About a dozen CS people stood around the dark wooden table. Chairs had been pushed back, and charts and maps covered the table from one end to the next. The CS seemed to have a lot of tech, but I was kind of glad they used paper too. It meant I could stuff something into my pocket if I needed to.

Nathan looked up from one of the maps. "We meet again. I can't believe you had a vision of the pilot. When in the world did you meet him?"

"More like where in the world," I said quietly. Louder, I said, "I guess I just bumped into him at some time."

Nathan gave me a funny look, like he wasn't sure he believed me. Still, he slapped me on the shoulder. "Another life, eh?" He gestured around the room. "Have you met everyone?"

Sarah hurried in with a tablet computer in her hand. "Introductions will have to wait. From the information we've pulled together, it's clear McKnight will die tomorrow in the middle of his part of the air show. McKnight's plane will crash into the crowd, or wreckage from it flies into the crowd. But we have a problem."

She put down her computer and pulled out one of the bigger maps. "Here's the setup of the fairgrounds. And here's McKnight's flight path." Pulling out a pen, she swiped her hand across one the map, drawing a thick red line. Everyone leaned forward to study it.

Hank Fallston stepped forward. He shot me a look,

and I edged back up against the wall between Colin and Lisa. Turning his back to us, he pointed to the map. "Air shows don't put flight paths directly over spectators anymore. And McKnight's path is no exception. There is no way wreckage could hit the crowd. McKnight's flying too far away from the grandstands. How is he going to kill at least fifty people?"

"Fifty?" I asked, the word stumbling out of me.

Fallston ignored me, but Sarah nodded. "We're getting calls from all over about this one. The vision count is so far at fifty-two. We can only assume the number of injured is going to be a great deal more than that."

Colin swore. A couple of people in the room, including Fallston, frowned at him. Colin waved a hand. "Sorry. It's just a lot people."

"So what are you thinking?" Archer asked. "More than one disaster?"

"At precisely the same time as McKnight dies?" Hank Fallston gave a snort.

Sarah straightened and gestured to Nathan. "Tell them your theory."

Nathan waited until everyone turned to him. A small smile curved up his mouth.

Colin leaned in close and kept his voice quiet. "He loves this."

Smoothing back his hair, Nathan gestured to the map.

"If a piece of McKnight's wreckage hits one of the planes on display at the fair, and that plane is fully fueled, the explosion, well, that could be the cause."

Archer shook his head. A short woman spoke up. "It seems too convenient, doesn't it? McKnight dies, and then seconds later, a large enough secondary incident takes out dozens of spectators?"

"What are you thinking?" Archer asked the woman.

She pursed her lips. "Can we rule out the possibility that someone wants to make a statement?"

"Terrorists?" Nathan asked. "In Abbotsford?" He didn't laugh, but his mocking tone made it clear he thought her idea was absurd. The woman shot him a glare.

"At this stage, it's not wise to rule out anything," Archer said. "First priority is to keep McKnight grounded. After that, we'll need to be on the scene, so why not look for signs that this isn't just an accident waiting to happen and that someone is targeting the air show for a reason?"

Sarah clapped her hands together. "You know what to do. Let's move. Oh, Dean, Lisa, and Colin, please stay behind a minute."

She sounded like a teacher asking us to stay after class. I looked at Lisa. Her face had gone pale, leaving her freckles standing out. I was sure mine had, too. Colin said under his breath, "Great. What have we done now?"

I didn't know, but I was sure we were about to find out.

CHAPTER 8

Most people filed out, but Sarah spoke to a couple of people, including Nathan and Hank Fallston. They stayed in the room with us. So did Archer and a couple others.

Sarah took a deep breath, let it out with a huff, and then turned to the three of us. "Archer has told us all about you, of course, but it's wonderful to put faces with names. I think we need to grab a few minutes for introductions."

Oh, good. Not in trouble. Not yet. I cleared my throat, but even so, my words came out with a squeak. "Thank you, ma'am."

An older man sitting off to the side asked, "What did he say?"

"He said 'thank you,'" Hank said, sounding unhappy about me being polite.

The older man harrumphed and settled back into his chair.

"Please call me Sarah. I don't feel old enough to be a ma'am yet ... although I probably am."

Archer chuckled at that.

I thought Sarah looked younger than my parents, but I guessed she was probably about the same age as Archer—in her early thirties maybe. Colin, Lisa, and I were obviously the youngest CS members by at least a decade. Was that why Hank didn't want us around? We were just kids to him?

The idea sat like raw pizza dough in my stomach.

I turned my attention to the older man. Dark age spots peppered his skin. Time had also slumped his shoulders and thinned his body. His scowl reminded me of my former neighbor, Mr. Utlet, and the memory of my dead neighbor didn't help my nerves.

Sarah started giving us names as she pointed at the other people. Elizabeth Chang, Thomas Hawkman, Armitage Beauren. Then she aimed a black remote control at the monitor behind her.

"We have a video introduction about you three for the benefit of our remote members and other CS districts. I hope you'll bear with us." The screen turned blue, and an image of Mr. Vidmar appeared. He seemed younger than I remembered. Beside me, Lisa drew a quick breath. Throat tight, I blinked at the screen.

Sarah turned to the others in the room. "As some of you know, young Mr. Curse came to us when Arsney Vidmar gifted him with the visions. This was after Dean came to Arsney's aid during a mugging."

Several people in the room nodded and whispered. I heard someone say, "Miss him so much." I glanced at Nathan, thinking he'd said that, but he stood with his back braced against the wall, his legs crossed at the ankles, and his arms folded over his chest. His jaw muscles tightened and twitched, yet he hadn't said anything.

Sarah gestured to where I stood. "Dean enlisted the help of his friends, Lisa Green and Colin Blane." Their photos popped up on screen, and Colin nudged me. "Not my best side."

I shook my head and tried to pay attention to Sarah.

"... no formal apprenticeship, our young trio has proven—more than once—their ability to apply their talents to our cause." I winced as grainy video taken from cell phones or security cameras showed what we'd been doing so far. A newspaper article mentioned Mr. Utlet's death. A clip, which must've come from Dimitri Vidmar, Arsney's brother, showed me jumping in front of a car to save my sister. A photo popped up of the man in the mall with the peanut allergy. And a short scene from the security cameras at the paintball battle showed me shooting a few of the kids. Obviously put in to lighten the heavy mood the video was causing. I groaned. I'd been having a vision at the time and hadn't meant to shoot anyone.

Colin didn't even try to swallow his laugh. Lisa smothered hers, and so did several others, but Nathan just turned to me and nodded approvingly. My face went hot, and I shifted on my feet, wondering how long this introduction would last and how long the CS had suspected me of having the gift. If they'd contacted me a lot earlier, maybe I could have saved a few more people. I shifted and pressed my lips tight.

"We have no privacy," Lisa whispered from between clenched teeth.

If Sarah heard Lisa's comment she didn't acknowledge it. Instead, she continued with the introduction. "Normally, when a member tells us they'd like to bring someone into the CS, we do a full investigation to see if that person can meet the demands of the Society. Our name is an accurate one."

Congregatio de Sacrificio—the Congregation of Sacrifice, I thought, shifting the name to English in my head. I figured these people had all given up a lot to be here. I wondered what Nathan, in particular, had given up. College maybe? Years of just having fun? He seemed young, but had he given up being a kid to be in the CS?

Would I have to also?

Sarah started talking again. "Once we realized Arsney had passed you his gift … well, I'm sure you can appreciate that if we'd swooped in, and if you had turned out to be less than helpful … you can see the problem we had to sort out."

So, after they knew I had the gift, they waited. Archer had said as much, but being reminded of the people I hadn't saved shoved a hot shard of anger into my stomach. I bit my tongue, although the words pushed out anyway in a rush. "Problem?" I asked, trying hard to keep my voice pleasant. "Just a problem, hey?"

I must not have done a very good job being cool because Colin whispered out of the corner of his mouth, "Take it easy, Dean."

Stomach roiling into knots, I shoved my fist behind my back. Colin was right. We were here to meet and make these people understand we could help. I *needed* that. But that irritation twisted and pushed at me. I kept thinking that the Society was playing around with other people's lives. It was a lot more than a problem to those who had died.

I clenched my teeth. Sarah and everyone else seemed to be staring at me like they didn't understand. It was only when I looked at Nathan that I saw someone who seemed to know how it felt when things didn't go right for you.

The words tumbled out before I could stop them. "I totally understand why you waited. My teacher, my neighbor, those people from the Gadget Emporium ..." I took a breath and let it out in a quick burst. "Sure, they all died because I didn't have a clue what was happening to me. They might have lived if you'd bothered to shoot me a quick note informing me that the visions I was having were of people who only had twenty-four hours to live, but, yeah, whatever ..." I gestured to everyone in the room. "You wouldn't want to risk compromising all of *this*."

I heard Nathan's quiet voice. "You go, kid."

I turned to him, but his face could have been a mask. He didn't show anything.

Archer cleared his throat with a rumble, although Sarah was the one who spoke. "Dean, we had no idea you had the gift before the incident with your neighbor. I'm very sorry. Once we knew, we put Archer on you. I certainly understand why you're upset. Everyone in this room appreciates what you've been through."

"Almost everyone," Hank Fallston said. He shook his head and stared straight at me. "You're untrained, and I wouldn't want my life in your hands."

Sarah locked stares with the man. "Hank, I thought we agreed I would handle this."

He met her look with one that seemed harder than the thick wood table in the room. At last, he nodded and walked out. The short woman named Chang stood up.

She came over and patted my arm. "You guys have done great. Frankly, I can't see anyone doing better with what you three had to handle."

"Couldn't agree more," Archer said.

"However," Sarah said, stepping forward, "there are a

few questions we must ask you now before we bring you, Dean, and Colin and Lisa, into our society."

My throat dried as if I'd swallowed sandpaper. I wondered who was watching us on the video monitor, and if what I'd said had made anyone think I'd be more trouble than I was worth. I nodded at Sarah.

She faced me and spoke slowly, the tone of her voice serious and the words formal. "Do you, Dean Curse, agree to keep secret the activities and structures of the *Congregatio de Sacrificio*? Do you agree to take every step possible to protect those people you see in your visions and the people seen by other members who may request your assistance? Will you act to save someone, thinking only of saving another soul, without any thought of gain or any belief that this makes you someone more powerful than others?"

I took a second to think about what they were asking. I really *did* want to help people. The visions had allowed me to save my sister's life. Maybe someday I'd save Colin or Lisa or even my parents. I didn't want to give that up. What if I saw a vision of my worst enemy? Would I act to save that person? I really hated Eric and Rodney, but what if I saw their faces in a vision? Would I think only about the goals of the CS?

Biting my lower lip, I considered everything. I knew I'd do it. I'd try to save them. And if I'd try to save even them, I couldn't think of anyone I wouldn't try to keep from dying.

I looked into Sarah's clear, dark eyes. I nodded. It felt important to do this right, so I said, "I will."

Sarah turned to Lisa and Colin. "And what are your answers to those questions?"

They glanced at each other and said at the same time, "I will."

"Brilliant," Archer said, rubbing his hands together.

Sarah nodded. "It is with great pleasure that I welcome you three, officially, as members of the *Congregato de Sacrificio*, Lower Mainland District, Abbotsford Zone."

Everyone applauded, except Nathan, who gave me a little two-finger salute as if in a sign of solidarity. Sarah switched off the monitor behind her.

"That's it?" Colin whispered to me, a little too loudly. "No clandestine ceremony with people in cloaks? No secret handshakes? Just a less-than-full office and a pat on the back?"

"There *is* a handshake, Mr. Blane, but it's not secret." Sarah beckoned us to her. The people in the room filed past, shaking each of our hands carefully. I finally figured out what all this was about. They wanted to touch us. I was connecting with them as much as they were linking up with me. If I was going to do something that would get me killed, I now had a lot of people who'd send me a message to let me know that I should watch it.

Nathan stopped in front of me. He didn't shake my hand and I assumed it was because he didn't have the gift, and maybe he felt weird about that. Or maybe he just didn't like me. He nodded. "Can't tell you how happy I am to no longer be the youngest member of our little group here. Good job slipping past old Fallston."

He stepped over and took Lisa's hand. "And really great to meet you. Let me know if I can help with any of your training. I'm a black belt, and I study three other martial arts, as well. I can give you a few tips."

"Y-Yeah," Lisa said, smiling at him. "You too."

Nathan left, and Colin shook his head. "What a clown!" He changed his voice to mock Nathan's. "Oh, I'm a black belt, and I study other martial arts, too, because I'm incredible." He sighed and shook his head. "He just blew me off like I was dirt on the floor."

Archer reached out to Colin. "Don't underestimate Nathan. He's smart. And he's had a rough time. His dad was a member, so he knows his way around the Society better than some members twice his age."

"*Was?* Did his dad die saving someone?" I asked.

Archer winced and shook his head. "Only in a manner of speaking."

"Then why doesn't Nathan have the gift?" Lisa asked.

"Why didn't he get it from his dad?"

"His dad died before he could pass his gift to anyone. Now's not really the time to dive into that."

Someone poked at me, and I had to turn. The old guy who'd had trouble hearing stood in front of me. He pushed his hand at me so I had to shake it. "Matthias Paulsen," he said, his voice rough as a gravel road. He gripped my hand. "I saw a little of what you did at the museum."

I swallowed. Saw? How? I glanced at Colin and Lisa and then back to the Paulsen. "Uh, I didn't realize ... I thought the thieves took out the cameras."

"Oh, they were out." The old man smiled. "We do have other sources, though. And the thieves weren't the ones who took care of the cameras. Didn't Archer tell you about the role he played?" He looked at Archer and shook his head. "Long story, all very technical. I'm sure he'll explain it one day. But I am curious. How do you justify destroying priceless artifacts, injuring innocent people, vandalizing property, and committing theft? Yes, I know all about that part of it too."

I jerked my hand away from him.

Archer came over and laid his arm over my shoulder. "Come on, Matthias. You know they saved lives that day."

The old man stiffened. "I am well aware of your policy about how the ends justify the means." His gaze moved toward the door Nathan had just gone out. "You're not the only one who thinks that. In my day, we didn't need to become criminals to save lives."

"That's enough, Matthias," Sarah said.

"Really? Are we even sure those monks were right about their claims to that relic from the museum? What if they were lying? Or mistaken? We just admitted a member who helped someone get away with theft. Have we become so hardened we now ignore laws?" Matthias looked at me as if I were a dog who'd just peed on his shoe. "You had a promising start, son, but that museum escapade ..." He shook his head. "I'm not sure Hank isn't right about you."

When Matthias left, Archer blew out a breath. "Sorry about that. As you can see, we have a few members who agree with Hank."

"He's right, you know," Lisa said. "We actually didn't do our homework on that one."

Colin glared at her. "Hey! We only had twenty-four hours and the people who were supposed to die are presently alive and well."

Archer lifted his voice. "And it's worth noting that I *did* do the homework. That ancient head is now back at the village where it was originally stolen from. I can even tell you how Sokum Pram connected with those thieves."

Sokum—Sok—was only a couple years older than me, and the youngest monk I'd ever met—not that I'd met a lot of monks before him. And I remembered how desperate he had been to get the stolen relic back to his grandfather's village. I was glad to hear that Archer had kept tabs on that situation.

Still, my hands shook, so I stuffed them into my back pockets. Excitement shivered inside me. A thousand questions tumbled through my mind about the CS. What I'd said played over and over in the back of my mind. Had I been out of line by telling the CS how they should have contacted me? Maybe Vidmar giving me the gift had thrown them as much as it had me? Maybe I should have kept my mouth shut.

Lisa must've seen something on my face or in my eyes. She stepped close and whispered, "I'm glad you said what you did."

I smiled at her. That made one of us. Looking at Archer, I asked, "So what now? Do we head to the air show? Go over plans?"

It was barely afternoon but I had a feeling we were in for a long day. I wondered what I would tell my parents. *Sorry, but I need to go save lives so I won't be home for supper.*

Dad would probably want to sit me down and have a long talk, and Mom would stick something on my forehead to see if I had a fever. They sure wouldn't let me stay out all night and all day tomorrow. Could I invent a story for them?

Thoughts kept spinning, but Archer started leading us to the front of the CS offices. "I'm taking you guys to the mall."

CHAPTER 9

"We're not buying equipment? We're not on a mission? You're really dropping us off at the mall?" Colin stared out of Archer's car at the entrance. People walked in and out, talking and laughing. I wondered how many of them planned to go to the Abbotsford Air Show tomorrow. A shiver slid over my skin—and not from my still-damp clothes.

Archer unlocked the car doors. "Might be a touch odd if I drop you off at home. I don't think you want your parents asking who I am."

"What about all this?" I said, gesturing to my clothes. They were mostly dry, but they were terribly wrinkled. And I still smelled like chlorine. So did Colin.

Archer shrugged. "I'm sure you'll think of something. Keep your phones handy. You guys have done a lot today. Get some rest and be ready. We'll need all hands on deck tomorrow."

We got out of the car, and Archer drove off. Colin pulled out his phone and started messing with it, probably downloading apps and getting it set up just the way he liked. Lisa had been pretty quiet in the car. She stood there now with her arms crossed and her forehead scrunched. She seemed really pale, as in, you could count every freckle on her face. "You okay? You look a little scared."

She swiped at her hair, pushing the loose strands back. I recognized her nervous tick and saw that her hands trembled a bit before she finally spoke. "I don't think I'm as scared as I look. But it's probably pretty close."

Colin weighed in. "Hey, I'm about as afraid as you look, too. My dad always tells me when you're shivering inside you need to start doing something to loosen up so you don't get frozen by the fear."

"Come on. Let's walk home. And this time we're going to do our homework on the way."

As we walked, I pulled out my phone and nudged Lisa to do the same. She shook her head and leaned over to look at my phone or at Colin's.

"Doris sent us everything on Karl McKnight."

Lisa grabbed Colin's shirt to keep him from walking into someone else. "It's like a full Wiki listing. The guy is thirty-nine. Lives in Melbourne, Australia. He's married and has a six-year-old daughter named Madeline."

We stopped at a street corner to wait for the light. Lisa's eyes went wide as she stared at my phone. "Wow. Doris really did get everything. His school and military records, hospital records—"

"Police records," Colin said, scrolling fast. "Guy was in a bar fight a decade ago and broke his jaw. So much for g'day, mate."

"Ouch," Lisa said, rubbing her chin. "Well, if you think about how much the CS knows about us, it's not surprising they have this kind of information about McKnight. How is this helping?"

The light changed, and we started walking again. Colin tapped his phone. "He's some kind of national hero down under. Former RAAF pilot, decorated war veteran. It's his first time at the Abbotsford Air Show." He looked up. "Do you think the CS has those zone things in Australia?"

"I bet they have them everywhere," Lisa said.

"Oh, sweet!" Colin held up his phone to show a photo of a silver plane with two red and black stripes running down the body. "Did you see what this guy flies? An F-86 Sabre."

Lisa cocked her head to the side. "Is that supposed to mean something?"

"Don't worry," I said. "He doesn't have a clue what it means either."

"Hey! First swept-wing jet the US ever made. Canada and Australia built their own versions. It was outdated in the late years of the Cold War, but it had a top speed of like six hundred miles, which is basically a rocket. An F-86 is like—"

A small, high voice cut off Colin's words. I jumped, and we all stopped when we saw Rylee Davis standing on the sidewalk outside of a taco stand. "Hi, Dean."

She smiled and walked over to us. The breeze blew a few loose strands of her brown hair across her face. My heart thudded up into my throat. "Um ... hi, Rylee."

She glanced from me to Colin, frowning. "Did you guys go swimming?"

"Training for a triathlon," Colin said. He gave her a firm nod. "We train fully clothed. Makes the day of the race a lot easier."

Oh, no way would she buy that. But I plastered on a smile like I believed every word he said. Rylee gave Colin a sideways gaze, as though she wasn't sure if he was lying or not.

Then Rylee glanced at Lisa. "You're not training?"

Lisa smiled but didn't say anything, which was a bit weird.

"So ... um ... how are you?" I asked.

Glancing back at the taco stand, Rylee said, "My mom's getting dinner. Y'know, I kind of miss our weekly meetings. Did I hear you're still going?"

Rylee had been going to therapy with us, but her mom pulled her out after the first few sessions. I'd overheard Rylee telling her friends that her mom thought therapy was for *really* messed up people and that if she kept going it would give her a stigma or something. That was silly, of course, and even Rylee had said it was. It sounded to me like her mom didn't really understand the point of therapy.

I bobbed my head. "Yeah, you know, it's good to talk about everything that happened."

She gave me a shy smile. "I don't remember you talking a whole lot before, but I understand needing to, that's for sure. And you had a lot more to deal with, what with seeing your neighbor get killed and then you getting hit by that car."

"Hit by a car," Colin said with a chuckle under his breath. "Classic Dean stunt."

That got a smile out of Lisa.

Rylee bit her lip. "Right, well, are you guys going to the air show tomorrow?"

I cringed, and then my skin turned cold. I did not want Rylee going to the show—not tomorrow, at least. I shook my head.

"Oh, not tomorrow, or not this year?"

"Not at all," I said.

"You don't you like planes?" she asked.

"He's got a fear of them," Colin said. "It's called aerophobia."

Rylee eyes went as big as an anime character's. "Really?"

"No, not really." I frowned at Colin.

Lisa leaned over to Rylee. "He's embarrassed about it."

I gave Lisa a hard scowl, but she just shrugged.

A car honked, and Rylee turned and waved. "It's my mom; I better get going." She flicked a strand of hair out of her face. "So you probably don't want to meet me at the air show tomorrow, hey?"

"Yeah, sure. That would be awesome ... I mean—no! No way. That's a dumb show anyway. There's this great 3-D movie out. I'm planning to see it tomorrow."

Lame, lame, I thought. Add to that I couldn't think of the name of a single movie that I could actually mention and maybe get Rylee to go and see instead. Rylee stared at me, her face scrunched with worry. I grabbed her hand. "I'll text you. How's that? You don't want to go to the air show anyway. It'll be too hot outside."

Her smile brightened. "Okay."

I let go of her when her mom honked again. She started to turn away, but I said, "Wait, I don't have your number."

She grabbed my phone out of my hand. "Cool cell," she said, tapping the screen. She handed it back, and said, "Password, please."

I'm pretty sure Archer would kill me for letting another kid even touch my CS phone, but I could not say no to this girl. I entered my password, then put my phone back in her waiting hand. Five seconds later, her phone chimed in her purse and she handed my phone back to me. "There. I sent myself a text so now we have each other's numbers. See you tomorrow."

As Rylee walked away, Lisa turned to me. "How are you going to explain to her that you're not going to the movies tomorrow but you are in fact probably going to the air show? And you're going there to try and keep a bunch of people from dying?"

I didn't know what Lisa's problem was, but I wasn't in the mood to fight. I decided not to answer and instead watched Rylee get into her mom's car.

Colin shook his head. "Man, I can't believe Rylee Davis is even giving you the time of day, let alone her phone number. She seems to actually like you. *You.* How crazy is that, right?"

Letting out a breath, I was almost speechless myself. "I know. I don't get it either. I also don't know what I'm going to tell her to keep her home tomorrow."

Slapping my arm, Lisa started walking. Colin and I trailed after her. She dragged out her phone and started punching at it, jabbing at the screen like she wanted it to tell her something good. "I'm sure you and Rylee will be magic together, but right now, she's a distraction. Can we focus on that homework? I do *not* want a repeat of what happened at the museum!"

"Hey, we're saving lives here. Rylee's a life too.

Anyone we can get to stay away from the air show tomorrow is one more save. Right?" I hadn't noticed Rylee in my vision, but that didn't mean she hadn't been there. There were too many people, and I hadn't really gotten a good look at everyone. Plus, I only had visions of people who'd die. There were bound to be even more people seriously injured. I felt a chill at that thought but forced it out of my head.

We crossed the street and headed down another block. Lisa looked up from her phone. "Sorry, Dean. I guess I'm just worried about … well, everything. I keep thinking about what Matthias said."

Colin stopped in the middle of the sidewalk. "Don't tell me you believe that old man?"

The breeze rustled the tree leaves overhead. Lisa stared up at them and back at her phone. "We caused a lot of damage. We injured people. We lied to the police. We stole."

I stepped up to her. "What do you want to do? Turn ourselves in?"

She lifted and dropped her shoulders.

Colin threw out a hand. "Time to reset the top priority. Stuff is just stuff. You can replace things. You can fix anything you break. However, you can*not* bring someone back to life. If that's not number one over everything else, then what are we even doing?"

Lisa turned toward Colin, her eyes bright and her face red. I cringed. She looked ready to tear into him, but her stare was still fixed on her phone. Her mouth hung open.

"What?" I asked, trying to see what was on her phone.

"Yeah," Colin said, edging closer too. "You look like you found naked pictures of your grandpa."

I punched Colin's arm. "Why? *Why* do you insist on putting those images into my head? I don't want to think about that."

"You have problems, Colin. Real problems. But so do we," Lisa said. "Look at this. Karl McKnight arrives here today at six p.m. That's still a couple hours away. So he's not even here *yet*. And, yep, it says it again: he's never been to Abbotsford before. So, Dean, you want to tell us how you had a vision of him if he's never been here and you've never met him?"

"You never touched him?" Colin said, sounding uneasy as he shifted his feet.

I let out a long breath. "That's what I told Archer."

"And you were going to tell us about this ... when?" Lisa asked. She narrowed her eyes and propped one fist on her hip. Colin stared back at me like I had leprosy and it might spread.

I threw my hands up in near defeat. "I've been trying to figure it out. Archer said McKnight was probably someone I bumped into at the hotel this morning. I just thought ..." I shook my head. "I had wanted Archer to be right. I hadn't wanted to really think a lot about this."

Colin scratched his chin with his thumb and forefinger. "That makes sense. Harrison Hot Springs seems packed with people from all over the place."

Pushing her phone into his face, Lisa shook her head. "Are you even listening to me? He doesn't get here for a couple hours. He isn't now, and certainly wasn't earlier today, at the hot springs." She tilted her head at me. "Can you have visions now of people you haven't touched?"

I stuffed my hands into my front pockets. I'd forgotten my windbreaker in Archer's car, and the day had cooled off. I wished I had it on now.

Colin gave an uneasy laugh. "That'd be weird. Dean could end up having visions of random people he's never met."

I imagined the bodies of the people I *couldn't* save piling up around me. What if I did just keep seeing deaths—dozens, hundreds, thousands of deaths? My stomach flopped. A cold sweat soaked the back of my T-shirt. I could see myself in some place for the insane with white walls and me lying on the floor having vision after vision, trapped in nothing but a gray world of dying strangers. I started to breathe fast and shallow. How could I deal with this? And how could I even think of giving this to two other people—the only way I could get rid of it?

Colin jostled me by the arm. "Come on. Let's go figure this out at my place. My folks won't ask why we look like we went swimming in our clothes, and I can put yours through the dryer. You guys can call your parents from my place to let 'em know you're staying over with me tonight. Sound cool?"

What would be cool would be to figure out just how my visions really did work—and if they were something the CS had never really seen before. I also wondered if Vidmar had given me his gift in a way that made it go all wrong.

I really had to find out some answers, but I was pretty sure I wasn't going to find them at Colin's.

His house sat back a long way from the street with grass and trees and shrubs in the front and a wide curving driveway made of concrete tiles that fit together like pieces of a giant jigsaw puzzle. It had that perfect-house look. Behind the driveway, three floors of bricks and glass rose up like something you'd seen in a fancy magazine. Lisa gawked at it every time we came over, and today I wished I could too.

We pushed through the oversized front doors and into an entry. Family pictures and framed movie posters of films I'd never heard of hung on pristine walls. Either Colin's mom had acted in each of the movies or his dad had worked as a location scout on the film.

From the next room back—the kitchen—I could hear Colin's mom humming, something bright and cheerful. As far as I knew, Mrs. Blane hadn't been in a movie for years, but to me, it always seemed like she was ready to step up and perform for us. I wondered if the stay-at-home mom role was something she pretended to do, rather than something she did.

"Colin, is that you?" she called out. She made the words into a singsong, her voice lilting and pretty.

"Hi, Mom," Colin yelled back, poking his head into the room. The kitchen sat just behind there. Lisa and I added our own calls so she'd know we were here too.

"Kids! Snacks in the kitchen—come and get them!" she shouted. She sounded like a commercial for something that tasted really good.

Colin motioned down the hall. "I'll grab food and meet you in my room."

His room was about twice the size of mine at home. It looked as photo-ready as the rest of the house: bed made, books in order on the shelves, a desk set up near the front windows, a couch and TV, dark navy curtains, and matching carpet. I knew the tidy room wasn't Colin's doing. The mess in his school backpack could make a homeless person cringe. But Colin had said his parents hired a cleaning service. I wished mine would. I had to face a weekly inspection, and if my room didn't at least have the underwear off the floor, I spent Saturday picking up everything.

I plopped onto the small sofa that sat in front of his flat-screen TV. His room was big enough that all the extra furniture didn't crowd it. Lisa pulled out the desk chair and sat down, her phone in her hand.

Colin's movie infatuation showed in the posters plastered over the walls like some kind of papier-mâché project. "An ode to every movie I've seen and loved," he'd said after we'd had to study odes and epic poems in English.

Back when he only had a hundred or so posters, it hadn't looked that cool, but now I had to admit, the layers had become intense. Plus, it brought back a lot of memories.

"Remember that one?" Lisa asked, gesturing to where half a poster from a spy movie peeked out. Colin had dragged us to that one a couple summers ago. Everyone in the movie spoke Russian, but English had shown on the screen as subtitles so you could read what they were saying. It had been interesting to see the Russian spy be the hero and the American turn out to be the bad-guy terrorist.

"Yeah, that's the one that had Colin saying *nyet* for *no* and swearing he was going to become Blane, Colin Blane, double-oh-seven."

"And look at us now," Colin said, walking into the room with a plate of chocolate chip cookies. He set them down on his desk beside his laptop. "Living a double life, having dangerous adventures." He pulled out his phone. "Gadgets even."

I had to grin at his assessment.

This was exactly what I needed. Me and my friends hanging out. It felt like forever since we'd sat around eating stuff that would rot our teeth and making each other laugh. Even Lisa was smiling. She needed this too.

Then all our CS phones rang at the same time.

CHAPTER 10

I answered my phone first.

Sarah Pickett's face came on the screen. "Dean, Lisa, Colin, I'm patching you into our update meeting."

Colin and Lisa came over to the couch, and we matched up our phones so we'd all be seeing the same thing.

Sarah kept talking to people in the background. I recognized a couple of faces from this morning, including Nathan. "For those of you who've just come into this, as you've been advised, visions have shown a major accident at the Abbotsford Air Show tomorrow afternoon. Current count from all members who had visions—which came from nearly half a dozen countries by the way—is sixty-seven spectators dead, including the pilot who sets off the event."

"Sixty-seven?" Colin whispered and then made a face. "We're going to be busy tomorrow."

On the phone screen, the view pulled back to show Sarah sitting in the CS meeting room. "We expect even more injuries on top of that. We also think the cause will be the pilot crashing into the crowd."

"We're not sure about the cause," Nathan said.

Sarah glanced to one side. "When you hear hoof beats, it's wise to think horses, not zebras."

"Unless you're in Africa," Nathan said, and I could hear the smugness in his voice. I was impressed he could be calm about so many lives being on the line. He sounded like it didn't even matter to him. I wondered if growing up with the Society had desensitized him to the stress of it all. Maybe visions and people dying became part of the day after a while. That thought calmed and frightened me in the same instant.

I noticed names had popped up on one side of my screen. I squinted at them and then saw the blinking light on my phone. A camera. Meaning Colin, Lisa, and I had to be showing up on the CS meeting room monitors. I became instantly self-conscious and slid my thumb over the camera to block out anyone's view of my face.

If Sarah or anyone at CS noticed, no one said anything. She continued. "We have two CS members showing up tonight as part of the flight crew. A car accident disabled the flight members who were supposed to arrive at the hanger. No major injuries, but we have a doctor on staff who will keep them overnight at the hospital for observation. By morning, we will know everything about McKnight's plane. His aircraft is also going to be grounded with minor problems. Just enough to take it out of service for the next forty-eight hours. Now, what's the update on getting the people in our visions to stay away from the air show?"

Several different people spoke, explaining that special deliveries had been sent out with complimentary movie passes and free dinner offers to some of the people identified. In the background, I saw Nathan shake his head. However, it was Hank who spoke up.

"Of course, this doesn't mean those people won't still try to get to the show. Additionally, McKnight might try to fly another plane. We've looked at options to close the entire show—we could call in a bomb threat. Needless to say, we have to be careful we don't cause even more panic and accidents. The CS is not going to start acting like a bunch of terrorists."

I winced. It seemed to me that calling in some threat that would keep everyone away from the fairgrounds would actually be a good idea. But the pilots might still fly, and the people who died might end up being the security staff who would stay at the grandstands. So maybe Hank was right.

Sarah nodded as if she agreed too, and said, "We want every available CS member to be at the air show tomorrow. We will connect with as many people as we can, touching those in the front rows so we watch for second visions. That will be the alert to move the crowd. Any questions?"

Next to me, Lisa cleared her throat. "I have one."

Sarah seemed to look directly at me, but I knew she was looking at a camera so Lisa could see her. "Go ahead, Lisa."

I knew with a sudden sinking feeling what she was going to ask. I wanted to jump up and stop her, but I knew I couldn't. Instead, I covered my eyes.

"How did Dean have a vision of Mr. McKnight when it's impossible for Dean to have touched him?"

No one said anything. Hank glared up at the camera as if he could see me, his eyes narrowed. Nathan cocked his head to one side. At least he didn't look like he wanted to reach through the phone and grab me. Sarah shook her head. "He had to have touched him, Lisa. There's no other way. At some point their paths crossed."

"Or he's lying." The muttered words came across the line, and I couldn't tell who had said them. Hank? Nathan? Someone else who didn't think I should be part of the CS? Would they use this to kick me, Lisa, and Colin out when we'd barely gotten in?

Lisa opened her mouth to say something else, but Colin kicked her foot. I cleared my throat so she'd look at me, and I shook my head. Lisa closed her mouth and kicked Colin back.

Sarah said, "There's a church a block from the showgrounds. You'll receive the address and meeting time in a text. Don't be late. A video of this meeting will go out to members in all districts as well. We're pulling in every available member, and we're going to have sixty-seven wins, people."

The call ended, and our screens went dark. Lisa, Colin, and I just sat and stared at one another.

Colin moved first, pushing up from the couch. "There's something wrong with that Nathan guy."

Lisa scrunched up her face. "Why? Because he's not sounding all frightened like we are? He's grown up doing this. He's been trained to do this. We haven't. Of course he's going to be calm and be able to act like this is just another day."

"Did you see him? He actually smiled when Sarah was talking about all the members being brought in."

Lisa got up and paced around a bit. "Yeah, I'm smiling about that too. We need all the help we can get. We're not used to being part of a team, but we have to start thinking like that."

I got up as well and got a cookie. I didn't feel hungry, but tearing it apart into crumbs gave me something to do. "Maybe he's excited to be involved in such a big mission. Or maybe there's someone from another district he knows and likes, and this means she'll be in town."

"Oh, like Rylee and you?"

I turned to Lisa, and we locked stares for a few

seconds. I didn't know why she was being so hard on me. What was it to her if I liked Rylee or if Rylee liked me?

Colin cleared his throat. "Okay, maybe it's just that I don't like this Nathan guy, but what about everyone getting all weird about how Dean had to have touched McKnight? Someone even called him a liar, and I think it was Nathan who said that."

I shook my head. "It was probably Hank. He doesn't think any of us should be in the CS. So we need to prove him wrong."

Colin tapped his phone to his chin. "I've been thinking."

"Uh-oh," Lisa said, rolling her eyes.

Colin ignored her. "Do you know who *I* think we should talk to?"

He sounded like he had just come up with another one of his half-baked ideas. I was afraid to ask, but did anyway. "Who?"

"Ms. Myers."

Lisa's mouth fell open. She shut it with a snap and asked, "Professor Myers? From the university? Between the way you drooled on her shoes and the way Dean left her office the last time we were there, I think it's best if she never sees us again. Ever!"

"Just because Dean puked in the flowers outside her office ..."

"Colin!" I made a *shut up* face at him.

My friend smiled and put on that voice he used to talk Lisa—and me—into almost anything. "Come on. You know she knows everything about secret societies. She knows Dean's folks—"

Lisa shook her head. "They all teach at the same university. That doesn't make them all best friends."

We'd gone to see Professor Myers before the CS made contact with us, just after we had started to think there could be a secret group who knew what had happened to me. I'd had a vision of my little sister a few minutes into our meet, and I'd run out, screaming and freaked out. I was pretty sure Professor Myers never wanted to see me again.

"She knew about the CS!" Colin said, as if that clinched the idea of seeing her again.

Lisa caught on. "She knew they'd been mentioned in history books. She didn't think they were real. In fact, she insisted they *weren't* real about a hundred times."

Colin raised a finger. "But she knew about them."

Huffing out a breath, Lisa shook her head again. Her ponytail swung this time. "We're getting off track. We need to be focused for tomorrow. And rested."

"Okay. Tomorrow we save the world. Or at least a lot of Abbotsford," Colin agreed. "The day after tomorrow, we have a date with a hot professor." He held up his phone. "I already texted her."

"You didn't!" I poked Colin in the chest. "You have to agree right now—no spilling any of the Society's secrets. To anyone. We can't talk about the CS in therapy. And we can't talk about them to anyone else."

Lisa chewed on her lower lip and asked, "Therapy? Don't we have to work in a visit to the museum before we see Dr. Mickelsen again?"

"Let's take this one day at a time," I told her. Colin agreed. We sat down to eat the cookies. His mom would be insulted if we didn't make them disappear, and they tasted even better than they smelled.

It was a little weird, knowing something big was about to happen but not running around and trying to figure out just what that something big actually was. Lisa was right. We weren't used to being part of a bigger team. Even this morning at the hotel, it had felt more like saving Mrs. Yamada was all on us.

We hadn't heard from Doris about Mrs. Yamada, and suddenly I couldn't eat any more cookies. I tossed the one I'd taken back on the plate. Colin glanced at me, but he snatched up the cookie and ate it.

Lisa shifted on the couch, drawing her knees up to her chest. "At least we'll have help tomorrow. It won't feel like we're the only ones at fault when someone dies."

"How many times do you need to hear it's never on us?" Colin asked her. "That person is going to die. We get to try to intervene. That's it. It sucks if we fail, but we don't kill anyone. Don't you get that?"

"You can really separate yourself from it? Like Nathan seems to?"

"Not like Nathan," Colin said, his eyes narrowing. "But, yeah, sort of. Look, every time we have a mission, I pretend I'm a firefighter. We're going to a fire … the fire is the person who's going to die and —"

"I get it," Lisa said, cutting him off.

"Right, well, when it doesn't go right, I imagine something slowed the fire truck down. Or maybe the fire was so big no one could have put it out. Either way, we heard the alarm. We responded. We did what we could."

"Is that what you do, too?" Lisa asked me.

Surprised by the question, I said, "I don't know. I guess, to a point."

Letting out a growl, Colin sat down on his bed. "You guys are going to go insane. Tomorrow a whole bunch of people who *were going to die* will probably live."

"It's the probable part that gets me," Lisa said.

From somewhere beyond the other side of the door, Colin's mom called, "Are Lisa and Dean staying for dinner? They're welcome to, if their parents are okay with it."

Colin gestured to my clothes. "We forgot to get you cleaned up."

I glanced down at myself and made a face. If we really

had to face a disaster tomorrow, I wanted to sleep in my own bed tonight. I wanted to see my folks. And even annoying Becky. I stood up. "I should get home."

But the truth sat like a knot in my stomach, and a voice in the back of my mind whispered, *You're going to fail. There's no way you and the CS have a chance at saving over sixty people.*

I was pretty sure I wouldn't be able to even eat dinner or get much sleep.

Something just felt off to me. And it wasn't just the weirdness of never having touched McKnight.

What was I missing?

CHAPTER 11

I was able to sneak into the house and get to my room before anyone saw me, especially Becky. She would have told Mom and Dad that I smelled like a swimming pool.

I should've been excited to be part of the CS. I had people who knew about my visions, and they also had my back. Or mostly they did. I kept thinking about Hank and how he was Sarah's boss and Sarah was Archer's boss. What if Hank decided I could no longer be part of the CS? What then? Could they force me to give my gift away, like maybe to Nathan or someone else they had trained? But why would they let me into the CS only to kick me out? That didn't make sense.

And where had I met McKnight?

At dinner, Mom asked if I was feeling okay, and Dad kept giving me funny looks. Becky kept talking about the air show and her collection of teeth, and I figured that was a good enough reason to leave the table early. I told my folks I was going to my room to play on the computer, but I spent the rest of the time before bed looking over everything on McKnight.

Again.

I went to bed early, which must've raised concerns with my mom because she came in and asked again if I was okay.

"Yeah. Just ... I think I ate something at the mall that didn't agree with me."

She nodded and smoothed my hair back. "Well, stay in bed tomorrow if you're not feeling better."

That sounded so good. Stay home. Let Mom feed me homemade soup. Watch stupid TV shows. No, I couldn't do it. "I'll be fine. I promised ... uh, Lisa and Colin that I'd go with them to the air—I mean, mall tomorrow."

"Mall? Don't you want to see the air show this year? Not a lot of time left."

I shook my head. "Nah, I've seen it a hundred times. Besides, I kind of told Rylee I'd text her about going out. And I don't think she wants to go to the show either." I cringed. That sounded like I'd asked Rylee out on a date.

Mom smiled and kissed my forehead. "Promise me you won't grow up too fast, Dean."

I nodded, but I had no idea how to make that kind of pledge.

That night, I tossed and turned, my sleep fraught with nightmares.

Airplanes flew in my dreams. They crashed, too.

I woke up with a start, hearing McKnight scream

again, seeing his skin melt off his face and char. I got out of bed, staggered to the bathroom, and splashed water on my cheeks. I leaned on the edge of the sink and took deep breaths.

At six a.m., I dressed and crept down to the kitchen. The house seemed quiet and dark around me. Colin texted me a few seconds later that he and Lisa would meet me at the bus stop so we could get to the CS meeting on time. After raiding the cupboard, I scarfed down some cereal. I wanted to duck out before anyone else woke. I dumped my dish in the sink and had turned to scribble a note for my folks when I heard the floor creak.

Turning fast, I expected to see Mom or Dad behind me. Instead, Becky stood there in her pj's, her hair pulled back in a ponytail, frizzy strands poking up as if she'd licked a dozen batteries. "Why are you up so early? You going somewhere?"

"None of your business." I headed for the counter and the notepad.

"Do you know my friend Jill?" she asked. Becky sounded nice, and that made the skin on the back of my arms tingle.

"No ... and I don't want to know her." I finished my note and pinned it to the fridge with a magnet.

"Well, she has a cousin who is visiting for the air show. Jill took her to see some of the sights in Abbotsford."

I stopped and stared at Becky. "That's really great. I'm so happy you're sharing this with me. I don't really have time for, you know, stuff I don't care about."

Becky stuck her nose in the air and went to the cupboard to pull out the cereal I'd just put away. "They went to the hot springs yesterday."

A lump stuck in my throat. I forced myself not to move. Not to react. A lot of people went there. It was a popular place. Oh, who was I kidding? I knew where this was going.

Becky got out a bowl and poured out her breakfast. When she finished, she reached into her pj's pants pocket and pulled out the cell phone she'd saved up two summers to buy. She tapped the screen and held it out to me. "Great video, hmm?"

The image on the screen jostled and focused on a pool. I knew what I'd see, but it still was weird to watch Colin jump into the water, and then me. The scene played out like I remembered, although it happened a lot faster than I remembered.

It wasn't so much that you could see my face. The video jerked around and showed my back more than anything. However, Colin practically looked right into the camera, and you could see Lisa's ponytail.

The video ended. Becky and I just gaped at each other. She didn't smile at me or anything. I had to give her credit; she knew she had me. But what was she going to do?

I blew out a breath and pushed down my shoulders. "Did you tell Mom and Dad?"

"Not yet."

"Then you plan to?"

"I haven't made up my mind. Who is that guy with you? I've seen him before."

Oh, yeah. Archer was in the video too. Becky had seen him when Archer had been parked outside my house, pretending to sell ice cream. I didn't want to have to explain him to her, so I went for my next best choice. "How about five dollars to delete that video?"

"It's already on YouTube, you know," she said smugly. "It hasn't gone viral or anything, but it could. Or someone might start sending out the link."

I forced a laugh. "A woman has a seizure, falls into the pool, and some people pull her out. You think that will go viral? Really?" I took a breath and lowered my voice. I couldn't have Becky start yelling back at me or else our parents would wake up and we'd be stuck here all morning talking about this. "It's not that interesting. So what if I happened to be there to help?"

"How did you *happen* to be there? It's two hours away. How did you get there? And who is that man?"

I leaned over Becky. "If someone put that video on YouTube, someone can take it down. Especially if someone owed me." That was cheap. I knew it. I felt a stab of guilt immediately for even saying it. But I didn't want that video going viral. I didn't want my parents to ask the same questions Becky had just asked.

I grabbed my backpack and pushed past Becky. She grabbed my arm. "Dean! We never talked about what happened at the park. You know—with the car. I never asked because I didn't want to think it was anything other than you seeing what was going to happen. You were on a hill. You saw the car and me running." She wet her lips. "I know I owe you."

I let out a long breath. I couldn't believe she picked now to bring up all this stuff. "Then keep your trap shut about this."

"I can't," she hissed at me. "It's freaking me out. How many have you've saved? You're going to end up in trouble for doing this."

I wondered now if Becky knew that I was going around trying to save people. When she was younger, she used to tag along after me. Had she been doing that again and watching? Had I been too busy with the visions to notice?

Eyes narrowing, she asked, "How are you always in the right place at the right time?"

I forced a fake laugh, but even I thought it sounded lame. "I'm not, trust me. It's usually the wrong place at the worst time."

"I don't understand. Can you ..." She lowered her

voice, and her eyes got huge. "Can you see the future?"

I groaned, although I was kind of surprised. Becky was Little Miss Scientist and beyond practical. Every time we watched a fantasy movie, she'd scoff at how unbelievable everything was. She already had her college picked out and planned to get degrees in like three different sciences. I decided to play on that. Eyebrows lifted high, I looked down at her. "Really? I thought you were smarter than that."

She blushed and let go of my arm. "I am. I mean, I don't think ... I just don't understand."

"That's because there's nothing to understand. Look, yesterday, well, Colin's dad went to Harrison, you know, scouting possible locations. Colin had to go to assist him, so Lisa and I went to hang out. Yeah, we happened to be there when this poor woman needed help, and that's about it. We split after the official emergency people arrived, so we didn't do anything."

Becky opened her mouth to say something but seemed to catch herself. She squinted at me. "That man in the video?"

"Which one? I saw like a dozen. I couldn't even tell you who was who. Now, look, here's that five bucks. Stop embarrassing me. I'm not some kind of hero. Dump the video and tell Mom and Dad I left them a note. If you really think you owe me, don't make them think I'm more nuts than they already do, okay?"

I turned and headed for the door. I didn't look back, but I could feel Becky staring at me, probably with that tight frown of hers. My skin itched, so I knew she didn't buy my story. She'd keep asking about Archer. She might even keep following me. I couldn't afford to have her at the air show today. I didn't want my folks there, either, so I'd only said in my note that I was hanging out with Lisa and Colin and I'd have my phone with me, that we might be at the mall or we might do something else like a movie.

Nevertheless, if Becky somehow found out where I was ... *not good*.

I needed a new plan.

CHAPTER 12

Colin and Lisa shivered in the cool morning air at the bus stop. Lisa had a sweatshirt on with her running shoes and jeans. She wrapped her arms around herself to keep warm. Colin didn't even have a jacket on, only a cotton shirt, jeans, and running shoes. He rocked up on his toes, and I figured he was too excited to be cold. I felt like I'd never warmed up after being soaked yesterday. The chill seemed to have crept into my bones and taken up residence. I felt old today, and I thought about my mom asking me not to grow up too fast. Seeing people dying wasn't going to help with that promise, and not saving them would help even less.

My life was getting way too weird.

I told Colin and Lisa about what Becky had said. "Which is why I'm late."

Colin grinned. "No way. I'm on YouTube saving that woman? That's awesome."

Lisa slapped his arm. "This is serious."

"I know, I know." Colin held up his hands, but he kept smiling, no doubt at the possibility that a video he had starred in might actually go viral.

The bus saved him from Lisa or me yelling at him. The vehicle pulled up in a puff of diesel and opened its door. We paid our fare and took seats at the back, passing the only three other passengers aboard.

Lisa lowered her voice so they wouldn't hear and asked, "What do you think we should do? Becky's actually pretty smart. Do you think she'll figure it out?"

I shrugged. "Dunno. I don't think she'll guess the truth, but she'll guess something. She thinks I was lying—and I was. Maybe she'll go to my parents with that."

"Maybe you should tell her everything," Lisa said.

Colin choked. He turned to her and said to her in a voice low, "Uh, the first rule of a secret society is that it's a secret. As in, this is Fight Club—you do not go blabbing to your little sisters that you joined it."

"I'm not talking about *blabbing*." Lisa played with her ponytail. "Honesty might be the best policy here."

"Oh, gag me." Colin faked a finger down his throat. "Did you just say that? Please tell me you did not just say that!"

The muscles in Lisa's jaw flexed, and I knew I'd better get between them before they got into a fight. "I'm not telling her anything. Becky might have her moments of being not quite so evil, but if I tell her, someday she'll only use it against me." I shook my head. "No, we're not telling her the truth."

Lisa swallowed hard. "Fine. Whatever. It's not like anyone at the CS actually said we had to keep it a secret, you know."

"Of course they did," Colin said. "It was just about the first thing Archer told us."

"No, he said the reason they'd waited so long to make contact was to see who we had told and to come up with a plan on how to handle that." She turned back to me. "Why don't you ask Archer or Sarah what to do?"

"I think you're wrong about that," Colin said. "I think it is a secret. A big one. But speaking of Archer and Sarah ..." Colin gave me a wink. "I think they're, y'know, *together*."

I stared at him. I couldn't believe what he was insinuating. "What? Together, together?"

He nudged me with an elbow. "Uh-huh. Didn't you see the way they were looking at each other at the meeting?"

"I thought I saw a spark too," Lisa noted.

I looked from one idiot to the other. "Really? And I didn't notice anything? Could that be because you two see hand-holding in every pair of people you see? You're both nuts. Besides, it's not any of our business. Now come up with some ideas for how I deal with Becky, and let's leave figuring out who likes who to the gossip shows on TV."

Colin and Lisa swapped looks like they were going to humor my bad temper. Sure, maybe I was a little stressed.

I couldn't keep my knee from bouncing up and down. I also was having a hard time eating anything. We batted around ideas—everything from stealing Becky's phone and hacking her YouTube account to paying for her silence to sending her off to China in a box. Why China, I don't know—that was Colin's idea. Even the cost of postage shot that idea down.

We got off the bus and made our way down the block until we came to the Church of Eternal Praise. You couldn't miss the place: large and white and gleaming in the sun. Stained glass windows covered the front of the building. A giant cross on the top of the pitched roof screamed "church" louder than any sign. The church sat across from the main gates into the Abbotsford fairgrounds. Big banners for the air show flapped in the morning breeze. Posters clung to the metal fencing around the parking lot and fairgrounds. No one had shown up yet, but you could hear airplanes droning in the distance. Some guy was driving a giant sweeper through the lot in preparation for the day's activities. There were vendors as well, who were setting up their booths, and food trucks already prepared for customers, casting scents out like fishing line.

Shading my eyes, I stared at the grandstands. They stood open on both sides and sat in front of a racetrack. The fairgrounds didn't just hold the fair. It hosted all kinds of events. Horse shows, concerts, and the air show. From where I stood, I could picture the grandstands burning. What would it be like with dozens of people caught in there? The screams. The cries. The desperation. The mess of broken bones and finished lives.

With a shiver, I headed toward the church. Colin ran up the front steps and tugged on the door handles. He pressed his face to the glass of the front doors. "It's locked. All the lights are off, and I don't see anyone."

Running to the far corner of the building, Lisa gestured for us to follow. "Over here," she said and disappeared at a run. We followed and saw a lot of people in the side yard.

Grass covered a strip next to the church before the area opened into newly blacktopped parking lot.

Archer turned and saw us. He wore jeans and a light-colored T-shirt, and the breeze ruffled his sandy hair. He looked as though he was dressed for a day off, or one being spent as a tourist at the air show. He waved us over, which made a number of others peer in our direction. We'd barely taken two steps before a slender woman with short red hair and a wide smile blocked my path.

"Dean Curse," she said. She held out her hand. "Great to meet you. All of you!" She turned and smiled at Lisa and Colin. "I'm Erin Doring. Seattle District." She snatched Lisa's hand next and shook it before grabbing Colin's and doing the same.

"Yeah, really nice to meet you too," Lisa said, backing up a step. She didn't look like she knew what to do with Erin's energy.

Erin simply grinned at us. "You three are the youngest members we've had in ... well, in forever. You're making history! I've been suggesting for years that we need to recruit younger people." She dropped her voice. "There have been a number of tragic incidents in high schools that might have been avoided if we'd had people on the inside."

A low voice cut over Erin's words. "That's one possibility." I jumped and turned. Hank Fallston glared at me. He held a paper cup of coffee in one hand. The steam seemed to curl around him like some kind of mist—or some kind of evil potion. "The other option is that someone so young isn't ready to handle this job. He might want to make up stories to make himself feel bigger."

Heat washed my face. I knew now that Hank was thinking I'd lied about my vision of McKnight or maybe that I was lying about never having touched McKnight.

"Mr. Fallston," Erin said, her smile dropping. She nodded to me and disappeared into the crowd.

Hank Fallston stared at me. "I'm going to be watching you." I didn't respond, and it wasn't as if he gave me the chance to because he'd barely finished speaking when he turned and strode away.

When I heard Sarah call my name, I turned and saw

her standing beside Archer. I blinked, realizing she looked a lot like an older, taller version of Lisa. She wore her hair pulled back in a ponytail like Lisa and had on a thin zip-up hoodie over a black T-shirt, jeans, and running shoes.

"Twinsies," Colin said, leaning over to nudge Lisa. She nudged him back, and we walked over to Sarah and Archer.

Nathan came up as well. "I knew you'd be here early this morning. Most kids your age sleep in so late we had a pool going about if you'd manage to get up on time."

"A pool?" Colin asked, frowning.

Nathan glanced at his watch. "As in betting on you. I just won twenty bucks on you, kid."

Colin braced his feet wider and folded his arms. "Ah, yeah, you know us *kids* these days. Getting drunk and robbing banks."

Nathan glared at him, his mouth pulled down like he'd bitten into something sour.

Lisa stepped between Nathan and Colin. "Do you think you have time to show me a couple of those martial arts moves?"

Nathan kept watch on Colin, but he said to Lisa, "Sure. No time like the present." With a smile, he took her hand and moved off. "Want to watch, Colin? You might learn a thing or two."

Back stiff, Colin nodded. "Sure. I'll watch." He leaned toward me. "Not sure I'll learn anything, but I'm not leaving him alone with Lisa." Nathan pulled Lisa with him over to a grassy area, and Colin followed.

Sarah came and took me around to meet a few people, but I kept glancing over to where Nathan was showing some kind of moves. He did something fast that ended up with him pulling Lisa's phone out of her hand. She seemed to pick it up fast because she did the same move on Nathan and then cheered for herself. He turned to Colin and made a *come on* gesture with his finger. I tried to pull away from Sarah, but she had someone else she wanted me to meet. I kept shaking hands, and when I turned back, I saw Nathan had dumped Colin flat on the grass. He reached out a hand, but Colin batted it away and stood up on his own. Lisa just shook her head like this was all Colin's fault, but I didn't think dumping a guy on his butt was a great way to teach anyone anything.

Beside me, Sarah called out, "Okay, everyone. I need your attention!"

Lisa ran over to me, and Colin followed. Nathan trailed behind them, smiling. I focused on Sarah.

"Thank you all for coming today and getting here so early. I know some of you traveled a great distance." She nodded to a slender man who leaned against the wall, sipping a mug of coffee. "Paul, could you tell us where we stand on McKnight's plane?"

"He's the guy acting as McKnight's flight crew

mechanic," Colin said. "I heard some of the others talking about him when we first got here."

Paul gave a quick nod to the group. "I won't bore you with specifics, but there's nothing wrong with McKnight's plane. Beautiful machine. F-86 Sabre. His regular crew knows what they're doing, but I made sure the plane won't fly today. A clogged line in need of replacement parts took care of that. The show took McKnight's performance out of today's schedule, but they'll have a new part later today, and he's set to fly tomorrow."

"Thanks, Paul." Sarah turned back to the crowd. "We'll know today if we've stopped the crash or whether taking McKnight's plane out of commission had any effect at all. Please be prepared. If all we've done is delay the event for twenty-four hours, you can expect your visions to be even more dramatic than they were yesterday." I could tell she was speaking directly to me, and I think most of the people in the group thought the same thing since a dozen glances were shot my way.

She rubbed her hands together. "And on that, I want to remind everyone that today's all about *connecting*. I want you to get out there and connect—touch as many people as you can. We have too many questions still. We know McKnight's plane is fine, and if we hadn't taken it out of commission, it wouldn't have failed. Plus, McKnight's flight path should not have caused anyone harm. Because of that, we can't rule out two separate events. Possibly related, possibly not. Be on your toes today, okay?"

"Smart," Nathan said under his breath. He noticed me and whispered, "Sarah's nothing if not thorough. That's why Hank lets her run this zone."

I shifted, and the hairs on the back of my neck started tingling. There was something in the way Nathan spoke—an insincerity that I couldn't put my finger on but wondered if I was just now hearing what Colin had heard all along. But Lisa liked him. I still wasn't sure, and I wondered if Mr. Vidmar had felt the same way—unsure. He could have gifted visions to Nathan a long time ago, but he hadn't. Why?

Sarah gestured to Archer, and he stepped up beside her, his expression unusually serious. "The plan is to gather at the grandstands at noon. Even if we've saved McKnight, it doesn't mean we've saved everyone else. A number of us have had visions, and if we can confirm that those people are all gathered in one place, and nothing else life-threatening happens today, we'll have confirmed that McKnight and his plane were going to be the cause of this tragedy. Until then, keep your eyes peeled. Follow your instincts. Record everything, and if you see something, follow up and alert others."

"I feel like we're about to be sent into the final half," Colin said.

Erin from Seattle heard him and shouted out, "C'mon, coach. Put me in. I'm ready!"

Several people laughed. Archer smiled and gave Colin an approving nod. I figured he was probably glad for the break in the tension. I was glad for the same thing.

With a clap of his hands, Archer said, "Okay, get out of here already."

Nathan said to me, "Text or call if you need a hand out there."

"We'll be fine on our own," Colin said.

Lisa turned her back on Colin and smiled at Nathan. "Thanks ... we totally will."

"No, we won't," Colin muttered.

Nathan snickered. "You're cocky. I like that. And I get that you want to prove yourself. I was pretty young when I started out. I used to feel like I had to show people I belonged. Maybe I still feel that way, but I don't mind you trying to take on the world." Then he added, "Just don't push me too far, okay?"

Nathan crossed the street and strode toward one of the entrances to the air show. Others had broken away from the group and were heading that way too. Colin steered us in the opposite direction from Nathan so that we walked along a stretch of sidewalk lined with people setting up tables to sell everything from sunglasses to sneakers. Photos of the pilots smiled up at us, some of them autographed. I thought about how Becky wanted to get her Bieber tooth signed.

Lisa grabbed Colin's arm and pulled him to a stop beside a man examining a table full of watches with airplanes on them. "What's wrong with you?"

Colin jerked his arm away. "What are you talking about?"

She leveled a cold stare at him. "Nathan! Why are you being such a jerk to him?"

"I told you. I don't like him."

I stepped between them. "Hey, guys. Could we not do this just now?"

Lisa huffed out a breath and jerked off her sweatshirt, tying it around her hips. The day was heating up and would be warm. "He's been nice to us, and like he just said, he knows what it's like to be our age and in ..." She glanced around us. "Y'know. The club. C'mon, Dean, back me up here."

"You were a little harsh," I said to Colin. "And Nathan is one of those who welcomed us into the ... the club."

"Thank you, Dean," Lisa said.

"But I have been wondering why Vidmar didn't gift him with the visions."

"Maybe he thought Nathan was too young?"

"Like Dean's old?" Colin shook his head. "I'll bet Vidmar had a feeling about Nathan too. I've got it. The guy's an actor, and I should know one when I see one. He's not even very good. He's about as genuine as that Rolex on the table!"

The guy selling the watches stabbed out his hand, pointing down the pathway when his possible customer put a watch down and walked away. "You cost me a sale. Move it before I call security on you."

"Oh, like you could afford any kind of cop looking at the junk you sell," Colin snapped.

I grabbed onto both Colin and Lisa and pulled them with me. We walked in silence the rest of the way to the side entrance. By the time we made it through the gate — past the metal detector, a bag search, and through a pat-down with a guard who seemed too friendly with my body parts — the sun had climbed above the trees. Sweat trickled down my back.

A breeze teased my taste buds with food truck goodies — sugary kettle corn, hot dogs, roasted ears of corn, fresh potato chips. Signs offered the things you couldn't smell, like fried Snickers bars on a stick. The gates had been open only a few minutes. A couple dozen people wandered past us, smiling and talking. Planes sat in the open areas around us — old ones and new ones. The canvas of the tents flapped between the planes, showing off flight patches and other items for sale. Displays fluttered with information on the various pilots who would be flying.

Every so often the noise of a plane taking off or landing buzzed in the background, but it was too early for any of the aerial shows. In front of me, a woman pushed a stroller holding a toddler, who banged a spoon on the edge of the metal with a ping-ping sound. The memory of my vision rushed back. I staggered.

Lisa's hand on my arm steadied me. "What is it? Did you see that boy in your vision?"

I shook my head. Not him. But if we didn't stop today's accident, if we only postponed it by twenty-four hours, I knew I would start to see the faces of those who would die the following day. However, the timing wasn't right. We had to hang around until this afternoon. I tapped my phone. The countdown app was front and center and practically screamed the fact that we had less than four hours.

Colin lifted his nose and gave a few huge sniffs. "I smell donuts," he said. "And chicken and cinnamon rolls and ice cream!"

"You can smell ice cream?" Lisa asked.

Colin gave her an incredulous look. "You can't?"

I rubbed my hands together. "Okay. Let's do this. Let's make some connections."

CHAPTER 13

We began our search at one end of the food trucks. No one really seemed to mind me bumping into them since the crowd was getting larger. I touched shoulders to slip past people. I cooed at babies and patted their fat cheeks. I backed into people and told them I was sorry. Next to me, Lisa and Colin had their cameras on to record all the faces. I didn't really recognize anyone, but it was hard to say who I had seen in my vision. Several stood out, but there were so many in danger that it almost didn't matter. But no one seemed to mind the contact since it was such a public event.

I kept touching people, my hands shaking every time as I braced for the worst. At least I didn't scare anyone by glazing over with any other visions. I wouldn't know for sure until later today since we had only a short time before any accident. Pretty soon we had our hands full of giveaways. People at the displays gave us flyers about airplanes and schedules for the shows. Around us, kids wandered past with melting ice cream cones and balloons shaped like airplanes.

Hours passed and it started feeling like I was walking with a weight on my shoulders. Colin stopped us under the shade of an enormous tree. Maybe he could see my shoulders hanging low or my feet dragging. I hunched over and hugged myself, trying to pull it together again.

Colin shook his head, but he didn't look at me. It was like he didn't want to see me starting to fall apart. "Okay, I have seen, like, nothing suspicious. Y'know, I heard what Archer said. But I think he's ... all of them are missing the most suspicious thing."

I eased down onto a wooden bench under the tree. "What would that be?"

Colin plunked down next to me. "McKnight."

Lisa nodded. "Yeah, McKnight is a bit suspicious."

Motioning for them to keep talking, I shaded my eyes with my hand. Colin braced his elbows on his knees. "You've never met him. You're sure of that. I'm sure of it. Yet you had a vision of him, and that's not supposed to be possible. So I want to see what happens when you shake his hand. You have to have some kind of connection with him. I bet it's something psychic."

"Oh, give me a break," Lisa said, fanning her face. The sun and heat had pinked her cheeks.

"You don't think we should meet him?" I asked.

She shook her head. "Oh, no, I want you to meet him too. But if you're psychic, I'm queen of the Nile."

"Denial, more like," Colin said. "I bet Dean saw McKnight in a dream."

Lisa shoved out her hand, fingers spread. "If it turns out you're wrong—which you totally are—I get to pick the next five movies we go see."

"Five? No way." Colin lowered his brows. "You'll pick chick flicks only."

"If you're wrong, I will. So how sure are you about this, Mr. Dean-Must-Be-Psychic?"

They shook hands, and I pushed up off the bench. Hoping they wouldn't notice, I rubbed the sweat off my upper lip. I was nervous about meeting the pilot but not because I was worried I'd have some kind of weird bond with him. I'd seen the guy die.

Not going to happen, I reminded myself. *His plane is out of service. He'll be fine.*

"Okay," I said finally. "Let's go find the Aussie flyer."

Before I'd taken two steps, I heard a familiar sneering voice. "Well, if it isn't the geek patrol!"

I turned to see Eric Feldman and Rodney Palmer standing way too close for my comfort. They blocked the path in front of us. I took a step back to get out of Rodney's cave-bear shadow. A guy that big shouldn't have been able to sneak up on a dead body, let alone us. He loomed behind his friend.

Eric eyed me like I'd crawled out from under a rock.

Eric always had to be the best. His jeans and sneakers showed off expensive labels. His sunglasses perched on top of his head like he was too cool to wear them. Even in the summer heat, Rodney had on a black jacket with zippers and chains dangling and glinting.

"Buzz-cut barbarian," Colin muttered.

Rodney didn't seem to hear him, and Eric was too busy looking me up and down. "Thought you'd be home hiding in the corner of your room with your security blankie. Or over at the museum like Dr. Mickelsen told you. Hey, shoot anyone today?" Eric held his fingers up like a gun.

He'd seen me make a scene with paintballs and me shooting too many people because of my vision. He was never going to let me forget it. "Shut it, Eric," I said. "In fact, why don't you and your pet here head home and give yourselves a whole day of rest?"

"I can see therapy's really been helping you," he said with a sneer in my direction. "Dr. Mickelsen will love hearing about how antisocial you're acting today. I'm here because of him, you know. And that means because of you. *Go out and meet some new people*, he says. Supposed to *practice good acts*, whatever that means."

"Figures you wouldn't know anything about that," I told him.

I was pretty sure Eric and Rodney had started going to

therapy because the teachers went easier on us. None of us had to write any of our finals, which was a good thing for Rodney. We'd skated out of school this past year, and I would bet Eric was hoping to keep doing more of that. He wasn't dumb, just lazy. But I was pretty sure Rodney was kind of stupid.

Lisa gestured to the two of them. "Oh, would you two just get lost, please?"

Eric leered at Lisa. "Woo-hoo, lookin' hot today, track star. Ever think of ditching these losers for some guys who'll show you what fun is really like?"

Lisa folded her arms across her chest. "Track star? Seriously?"

Stepping closer, Colin said, "She would, Eric, she really would, but Lisa has this rule about not hanging out with shrimpy punks."

Eric's mouth pinched tight. He straightened and strained upward, but Colin still had an inch more height. "Careful, Blane. Wouldn't want to get blood on your shirt."

Rodney raised his hand to either hit or shove Colin. Before Rodney could do anything else, one of the guys working the showgrounds called out, "Is there a problem?"

We turned to see a security guard who seemed all of seventeen years old. Scrawny and a head shorter than Rodney, he didn't appear as if he'd last five seconds if Rodney decided to make trouble. But Eric nudged

Rodney's shoulder. "C'mon, I saw Rylee earlier. Let's see if we can find her."

Panic sizzled through me. Rylee? She was here? I remembered I'd said I'd text her about a movie, but I hadn't. She hadn't waited for me, and now she was at the air show. "Go home, Eric. This is not a good day to be here. Trust me. I'm doing you a favor."

Eric shot a rude gesture into the air and strolled away with Rodney.

Lisa asked, her voice quiet, "Are they going to be in the accident?"

I couldn't say for sure. "It was hard to focus on any one person during my first vision. The pilot was the only one I really remember, but those guys weren't on the list."

"Oh, I have to show you something," Colin said. He held up his phone. He tapped the screen a couple times and turned the display to show a map with a blinking dot. "That's Archer's location. I downloaded a custom app that lets me ping the GPS coordinates of any other, uh, CS phone. You want to see where Nathan is? Or Sarah? I figured they watch us all the time. Maybe we should turn the tables a bit."

I put a hand over Colin's phone. "I think Lisa and I both have enough of an issue with the CS pretty much being able to spy on anyone, anywhere, without us spying on them. Come on, we need to find that pilot."

We headed for the hangars that had been set up behind the grandstands.

The VIP seats gave attendees a shaded area to watch the air show. People were gradually heading that way since the stunt flights were due to start soon. Behind the stands, tents stretched out in temporary hangars for the pilots and their planes. We saw planes lined up there for takeoff. Fuel trucks stopped by the planes on the runway, and mechanics in coveralls hurried around, looking after the planes. The runway was a distance away, but the fuel trucks returned to a station pretty close to the grandstands.

I wondered if we'd have any trouble getting in. A fence ran around the hangar area, with only one gate on this side. A security guard stepped forward, but Colin flashed his phone and the man waved us through.

"Okay, what did you do?" Lisa asked.

Colin smiled and showed her his phone. She snickered. Colin turned his phone screen toward me. "A VIP ticket?"

"Gold pass. But I didn't do anything—it's from the CS. Check your phones. I think they sent them to everyone."

Lisa and I both checked, and sure enough, we had special tickets, too, that would let us in to any area of the air show. "Cool," I muttered.

We strolled past the hangars like we owned one of the planes here. I hung on to my backpack with one hand

and my phone with the other so Lisa and Colin wouldn't see my shaking fingers. My insides felt like they'd been stuck in one of those cotton candy machines that swirl around and around.

Still no McKnight. No F-86 plane with the black and red stripes. I fiddled with my phone and pulled up a photo of McKnight and his plane, as if I didn't have his face burned into my memory. But messing with my phone gave me something to do. And then Lisa nudged my arm, and Colin stopped in his tracks, almost making me bump into him.

In front of us, I saw McKnight, just like he had been in my vision, wearing flight gear and sort of a uniform with patches. Lean face and a wide, smiling mouth. Sharp eyes. He placed a hand on his plane. A lady stood nearby holding a little girl by the hand. The girl broke free and skipped over to McKnight, and he scooped her up, so I knew she must be his daughter.

A couple stood in front of McKnight, taking his picture. And right next to them I spotted a familiar figure. As I watched, Nathan turned and gave me that two-fingered salute he liked to use. I stayed where I was, unable to move.

He strolled over to us. "I see you found the action." Nathan smiled and nodded at McKnight. "So far, so good. I've disabled the fuel pump on McKnight's plane."

Colin stared at Nathan. "I thought that guy Paul

already disabled the plane. That they're waiting for a part?"

Nathan's smile froze, but he lifted a shoulder as if it didn't matter. "Hey, anything that keeps him on the ground, right?"

"So you know all about airplanes now?"

"Colin," Lisa said, her voice low.

"No, it's okay. It's good to learn about each other's skills. Everyone in the CS needs a wide range of talents. I'm working toward a pilot's license—fixed-wing and rotary."

"As in a helicopter?" I asked.

Nathan seemed smug. "You never know what kind of skills you might need. The *Congregatio de Sacrificio* sends us into various situations and places."

Lisa looked around. "Uh, should you really mention that name here?"

"I know. Dumb name. But it's tradition. The CS isn't much better, but at least you could tell people that means something like Citizen Safety or Confirmed Sightings," Nathan said. "The whole secret thing, that's another tradition that gets in the way more than it helps."

"What do you mean?" I asked.

He nodded to McKnight. "Wouldn't you rather go over to him and just tell him you had a vision of him dying so he could change his own possible future to a better one?"

Colin gave a snort. "He'd think I was crazy."

"He wouldn't if he, and everyone else in the world,

knew about the CS." Nathan spread out his arms. "Think of it. You'd be better than the FBI—you'd be trusted, honored. People would go out of their way to be nice to you because you might save them someday. The world would like us if they knew about us. All this secret stuff, it's just getting in the way."

"But you keep things secret," Lisa said. She sounded about as worried as I felt. Was this why Vidmar had never given Nathan the gift? Because he didn't really believe in the CS?

Nathan gave a laugh. "Sorry. Got on my soapbox, didn't I? The things I would change if I ruled the world. I better go and touch base with Hank and Sarah and let them know we're good for today at least. Hey, you guys want something to eat? I'm buying."

I started to say no, but people crowded around McKnight now for his autograph and more photos. I wasn't sure I'd be able to even get close enough to touch him. Lisa, Colin, and I followed Nathan to the food trucks.

He bought us all chicken skewers and lemonades. I'd just bitten into my meat on a stick when I heard Eric's voice from the next truck over. It sounded like he was teasing someone. I couldn't hear everything, but I could hear the sneer in his words. "Oh, don't be such a crybaby."

I put my chicken back on the paper plate. Then I heard Rylee say, "Stop it, Eric. Stop!"

CHAPTER 14

Fists bunched tightly, I headed for Rylee. I felt my pulse tapping in my neck, and my face started to burn. If he'd hurt her ...

Pushing through the crowd, I saw Eric standing next to Rylee. He had her purse in his hand and held it away from her. She appeared red-eyed and scared. I called out Eric's name, and he turned to face me. Rodney stepped in behind his buddy for support.

Ignoring Rodney, I squared off with Eric. But I said, "Rylee, what's wrong?"

She gave a small sniff. "He just won't give me my purse back."

"Oh, come on. I said I was buying you lunch."

"Give her purse back."

Eric shoved Rylee's purse at her, and she took it, her hands shaking. "I'm still buying you lunch!" he told her. "And you ... you can just butt out." Eric shoved me.

I heaved him back. He came at me with a fist pulled back, yelling for Rodney. The next thing I knew, Nathan stood in front of me in what looked like a martial arts stance, and both Rodney and Eric were sprawled on the ground. Then he said to me, "You okay?"

"Uh ... yeah."

Rylee clutched my arm. "Thank you, Dean." She kissed my cheek. I felt my face grow even hotter.

Nathan gestured with one hand for Eric and Rodney to stand. "You boys need to go home."

"But we haven't even seen—"

Nathan lifted his hand, cutting Eric off. "Not another word. Get out or we have round two."

Eric scrambled to his feet. Rodney pushed up and lowered his head like he was thinking of charging at Nathan. Eric put a hand on his arm. "Tomorrow. Fine. I'll make sure my dad—and yours—hears you're hanging out with gangs now."

Moving fast, Nathan grabbed Eric's arm and twisted until Eric cried out. Rodney swung, and Nathan grabbed his fist with his other hand. I pushed Eric away from Nathan and faced him. "Let them go. It's not worth the trouble. We have bigger worries."

For a minute, Nathan just stared at Rodney, his eyes cold. He gave a small nod and let go. He held up a finger. "Don't push me, kid. Now get out of here."

Muttering, Eric stumbled away. Rodney followed him. Nathan turned to me. "I'm going to make sure those two leave. Your girlfriend okay?"

"She's not my girlfriend. I mean, she's a girl and a friend, but not—"

"Got it. Buy her a soda or something."

I moved over to Rylee. "What are you even doing here?" I pulled her hand off me. "Didn't I say today wasn't a good day for the air show?"

Rylee blinked hard, hurt showing in her eyes. "You said you weren't going, but here you are, and you didn't text me."

I pulled in a breath. "I meant to. Really. I did. But ... stuff came up."

She lifted her chin in the direction of Colin and Lisa. "I see. You wanted to hang out with your friends, not with—"

I took her hand. "Rylee, can I call you? Next week? Uh, we could talk. Would you stay away from the air show until then?"

"Next week it'll be over. You want someone to just sit and wait for you, is that it?"

"No, I—"

"Never mind, Dean. Thanks for helping me with Eric and Rodney, but I think it's better if we just—" She shook her head and walked off. I gave a groan.

Colin came over and tapped my arm. "Your chicken's getting cold, and your lemonade's getting hot."

I glanced back at the food. I wasn't hungry anymore. "Let's go meet McKnight."

At least the crowd around McKnight's hangar had thinned out. We poked our heads inside and saw a few guys sitting around playing cards. I didn't see McKnight, but his wife stood near a small office, talking on her cell phone.

The little girl I'd seen earlier skipped over to me and held up something that looked like a brick. "Wanna see my walkie-talkie?" She had an accent that made her a little hard to understand. I smiled at the girl. She looked like a storybook character with long, gold hair and a white dress. But she had chocolate smeared over her face and her walkie-talkie too. I reached for it, but she pulled it away. "It's special."

Besides her accent, she had a speech problem. A lisp made her *S*'s come out with a hiss. Lisa bent down next to her. "Hi, I'm Lisa. Why is this special? Does the chocolate make it that way?"

The girl shook her head. "You're funny." Looking up at me, she grabbed my hand. I braced for a vision, but nothing happened. The girl tugged on me. "Talk to my da."

"Da?" Colin said. "You mean your dad?"

"That what I said, my da!" She pushed the walkie-talkie at me. "I talk to him when he's flying."

My heart skipped a beat. "Is he flying now?"

"No, dummy." She smiled wide. "I'm Maddie. Who are you?"

"I'm Dean. That's Colin. And you know Lisa. Where's your dad, Maddie?"

"That's my mom." She pointed to the woman on the cell phone.

"Yeah, we know that," Colin said. "But where's your dad?"

With a shout, she pushed away from us. "Daddy! Talk to me on my walkie-talkie!"

McKnight stepped into the hangar and swept up Maddie in his arms. He kissed her cheek. "I'm not flying, sweetie. You have to talk to me tomorrow to wish me luck." McKnight spoke with an accent like his daughter. He started to walk over to his wife, and I knew I had to act.

Reaching out, I grabbed McKnight's arm. "M-m-may I have an autograph?" The words staggered out with a stutter, and the look McKnight gave me told me I must seem like a nutcase. Luckily, Lisa pulled out a souvenir program of the air show, and Colin shoved a pen at me so I could give it to McKnight. He smiled and signed the program.

He handed me the program and walked back to his wife and to Maddie.

I let out the breath I had been holding.

Lisa let out a sigh as well. "That is the cutest little girl."

"And the dirtiest," Colin said. "I think her chocolate ended up on my pen."

Lisa pleaded with me. "We have to save him—for Maddie! We have to."

I nodded, but I was sure of only one thing: I had never met McKnight before today.

We headed back to the grandstands to meet the others. Nathan joined us there and shook his head. "We need more CS members here."

It seemed like we had a lot, but maybe not.

According to the countdown we were in the final seconds—what had happened to the time? McKnight was grounded—we'd just confirmed that—but still my pulse quickened, and tension rose around us. I could see CS members bracing. I noticed Archer in the crowd, looking ready to move. You could easily spot someone from the CS—anyone not staring up at the planes was CS.

I checked my phone, and Colin whispered. "Five, four, three, two—"

"Could you *not* do that!" Lisa said in a hiss.

"Done."

Countdown was over. No accident.

He let out a whoop.

I wished I could. But I couldn't shake the uneasy feeling this wasn't done. I just about heard the group breath let out by the CS members. Archer came over to us. "Can I give you guys a ride home?"

The three of us followed Archer out to his car, which

he had parked next to the church across the street from the grandstands.

I waited until Archer dropped off both Lisa and Colin, and then I asked, "Is it really over?"

Archer's mouth flattened. I'd been hoping for a smile.

"You can't spread this around—not even to Lisa or Colin. We're worried, Dean. The CS has secretly had every aircraft being flown checked for flaws. We're looking into the medical backgrounds of the pilots, having CS doctors check them at the air show. We're monitoring weather reports. We're even checking for sabotage. So far, everything looks fine."

"Why do I hear a big *but* coming?"

"No one reported any second visions," Archer said.

"But you feel it too?" I slumped in the car seat. "It's like a cloud hanging over us. There's something else going on. I didn't have any second visions, either, but I ... the other times, when I saved someone, it felt different. It felt like it was over. This ..." I let the words trail off. I didn't know how to explain the skin-crawling feeling I had. It was worse than showing up for a test knowing I hadn't studied.

Archer pulled up a block away from my house. "Get some rest. We're going to keep on this until we're sure we have stopped any kind of accident."

I nodded, got out, and walked home.

By the time I got there, I'd made up my mind. I'd spend

the rest of the week at the air show. I had to make sure I'd done everything possible. If I stayed home and something happened ... I just couldn't face that thought.

Mom had dinner on the table. I poked at it and told her I'd eaten at the air show. She told me to at least eat my vegetables. I pushed them around and finally worked up the nerve to tell them what I knew they'd find out anyway. "I can't make the session with Dr. Mickelsen this week."

Simultaneously, Dad and Mom asked, "Why?" I knew neither of them was happy.

Pushing my food around on my plate, I glanced at Becky. She sat at the table with a spoon holding mashed potatoes in her mouth. My parents were waiting for an answer. What should I say? *I have to stop people from dying, but I'm not even sure they will now?* Not exactly great dinner conversation.

"It's just this week ... uh ... it's a second session in a week and I don't even really *need* to go. I just ..." I ran out of words again.

Dad put down his fork and folded his hands in front of him. I knew that meant he was really serious about this. "Dean, I thought you wanted help."

"I do, but ..."

Mom reached out and put her hand over mine. "Is it Eric? Is he causing trouble for you?"

I shook my head. "No more than usual. But ... I ... well,

Dr. Mickelsen gave us this assignment to go back to the museum. And we haven't gone yet. We haven't worked up the nerve. I can't go back to therapy until we do that, and I, you know, need to write down my feelings like he said."

Becky stared at me, and I could swear I heard her snort, but she dug up another spoon of mashed potatoes and put it in her mouth.

Mom patted my hand. "I'll take you to the museum tomorrow."

"No!" I almost shouted the word. Becky's spoon clattered onto her plate. "I mean, I have to do this on my own. Dr. Mickelsen talked about us having to face our pasts." I bit my lower lip. Did that sound lame or what?

Mom and Dad swapped looks, and I could see a long *Dean, we need to talk* meeting coming. If only I could put it off a few more days, at least until the air show was over. "It's not easy talking Colin and Lisa into this, but I think they should be with me since we all got into this together."

Dad pressed his lips really tight until they almost disappeared. But he and Mom both nodded. I offered to help clear up dishes, which got me more strange looks from my folks. Becky kept watching me like she knew I was ducking her. After dinner, I locked myself in the bathroom to avoid her.

Sitting on the edge of the bathtub, I texted Colin and Lisa.

COME OVER. NOT DONE YET.

I hid out until Colin arrived. Lisa showed up five minutes later, and I took them to my room. We were all a little squashed, and it was either sit on the floor or my unmade bed. We spread out on the floor.

I told them what Archer had said. "But don't tell him I repeated it. I'm not supposed to tell you, but I don't see why I shouldn't. I just don't think Archer wants everyone knowing everything."

Colin said, "He doesn't want Nathan knowing."

Lisa pulled out the pillow she'd been sitting on and hit him with it. "Will you stop that?"

"Only if you stop," Colin said, rubbing his arm.

"Fine. Truce," Lisa said.

"Good." Colin pulled out some papers he'd printed off. "I've been doing a little night work this evening. This is the flight plan for McKnight. It puts him over a small section of woods for his stunts." Colin pointed to part of the map.

Lisa asked, "Where are the grandstands?"

Colin moved his finger to a square on the map. "Here."

"That really is a long way away from those woods."

"There's got to be something else going on," I noted. "How could McKnight cause so many other deaths when he's not flying over where everyone is watching?"

Colin looked up from the map. "The one thing we keep coming back to is that you had the first vision of just McKnight—only you had it and only McKnight dies in it. That's got to be the key to everything."

I sat back, my hands braced on the floor behind me. "But did I really? What if that vision was just stress coming out?" I knew it didn't work like that. I was grasping and hated that I felt so desperate.

"Did it feel like that?" Lisa asked. I shook my head and wasn't surprised by what she said next. "Okay, then it's not that."

Warmth tingled in my chest. Even if I wasn't sure I believed in myself, Colin and Lisa did.

Colin said, "I don't care what that Hank guy says or that old guy or anyone at the CS—"

"Nathan seems—"

"Don't start that again!"

Colin and Lisa locked stares. She looked away first and nodded. "Sorry. My bad. But I was just going to say he seems to like Dean."

"Guys, can we get back to what we are going to do tomorrow?"

Colin said, "Wear your hiking boots. We're going to scout the woods."

The idea sounded easy. But it turned out to be harder than we thought.

I'd fallen asleep right after Colin and Lisa left. I didn't dream. I don't even think I moved. I woke up stiff, my pillow covered in drool, and Becky pounding on my door telling me to get up for breakfast.

In the kitchen, Becky watched me like I was going to steal her cardboard box of teeth. She had it out sitting on the table as she wrote out more labels. I asked Mom, "Does she have to have them around when we eat?"

Mom ruffled my hair. I got out of there fast enough that Becky couldn't follow without leaving her tooth collection behind. I heard Mom telling her to be sure to put them away where they'd be safe.

"Yeah, from me," I muttered. If I got the chance, I'd bury the entire box.

CHAPTER 15

I met up with Colin and Lisa, and we rode the bus out to the fairgrounds. We got off one stop early and headed for the woods.

The woods were really just a bunch of pine trees and oaks. They grew in a clump like someone had pushed them together and left them in a thick group. They screened part of the fairgrounds from the road, and the air show looked to be using them to shade a lot of the trucks that fueled the planes. They were parked in a line, and we could smell the jet fuel. I also spotted the poison oak right away: small bushes with some bright red leaves.

I pointed the poison oak out to Colin and Lisa. "Don't touch it unless you want to itch for a month." I'd made that mistake once at summer camp.

We went around the poison oak and headed deeper into the woods. Branches scratched my arms, and I heard Colin curse and slap at mosquitoes.

Lisa scolded, "Didn't you put on sunscreen and bug spray? What kind of spy are you?"

"One who does his best work in cities," Colin told her.

He slapped his arm, trying to squash another bug.

His slap echoed around us like a shot. Overhead, a group of birds took off. Black and small, they circled three times and came back to settle in the treetops again.

I stared up at the birds and then wondered if we were walking on a lot of bird droppings. I looked down to check and saw the footprint. "Hey, guys?"

Colin and Lisa stepped up beside me. "Is that your print?" Colin put his shoe next to the footprint, but the mark in the soft ground was a lot longer and more narrow.

"It's not mine, either," Lisa said, bending her knee to hold up her foot. "My shoes have special tread marks."

"Well, it's not mine." I bent down to touch it. The edges seemed soft, meaning it wasn't that old. "Hikers, do you think? Someone out for a stroll here?"

Colin swatted at another bug biting his neck. "I don't think anyone would come out here for fun—bugs, poison oak, and them." He glanced up at the treetops where the birds had settled and chattered away now like they were yelling at us for bothering them.

My CS phone beeped. So did Lisa's and Colin's. The sounds sent the birds up into the air again. We all checked the text message that came in from Archer.

MEET ME AT GRANDSTANDS.

Lisa twisted her head. "How do you think he knew we were here?"

I shrugged. "Maybe he thinks we're at home and will be meeting him here. Or maybe he's got an app like Colin's and he can track us with our phones."

Lisa shivered. "I'm not sure I like that idea."

"Hey, it's only CS members tracking other CS members. What's the big deal?" Colin asked.

We fought our way out of the woods and over to the grandstands. Today, it seemed even more crowded than yesterday, and I noticed a lot more people bumping into each other—CS members making connections. Archer ended up finding us. One minute we were looking for him, and the next, he just seemed to be there.

"Peanuts?" he asked, offering a couple of bags.

I took one since I hadn't had much for breakfast. Colin pushed his hand into my bag and took about half. The nuts were still warm and salty, and I started cracking and eating.

"Hey, there's Nathan." Lisa gave a wave. I saw Nathan right away in the nearby crowd. He gave me his two-fingered salute. I wondered if he wanted me to give one back, but I only nodded. Nathan went back to watching the crowd, but he didn't move away from where he stood by one of the giant pillars that held up the grandstand roof.

"Is McKnight flying today?" Lisa asked.

Archer shook his head, but he kept watching the crowd. "We faked a phone call saying his wife and daughter were in a car accident. He's on his way to the hospital and won't perform today."

"That seems a little mean," Lisa said.

Archer glanced at her. "Better a small scare for him like that than a big accident for a lot of people. There's been a lot of talk in the CS about the means we use to avoid accidents. A lot of other people think like you, Lisa, and don't want the CS doing anything that's ... well, maybe not a hundred percent honest. But if I had to balance a rulebook against a life, I don't see that as a hard choice. It's like the tech we use at the CS now. Whatever lets us get the job done is a good thing, and the CS is going to have to keep adapting and changing to keep up with our members, and our visions."

I nodded. To me, what Archer was saying made sense. But I could see how people like Hank might not want to change. My dad always said the need to change and the will to change were two different things.

Archer led us to some chairs, and we sat down. Colin stole the rest of my peanuts, and I started looking around to see who else was here from the CS.

Lisa kicked the leg of her chair and turned to Archer. "How'd you get into this, anyway? How'd you get the gift?"

Crumpling up his empty peanut bag, Archer threw it and landed it in a trashcan. He shifted on his chair, and I thought it wasn't just because the wood was hard. "It's not actually a good story."

"Are there any good stories?" I asked. "We deal with people about to die, so not too much funny stuff."

"Besides," Colin said, brushing the peanut shells off his jeans, "we need to know more about you. Heck, about everyone in the CS. Don't we?"

Archer stared at the crowd around us. He looked from me to Colin to Lisa and back to me. Sitting up, he cleared his throat. "Do you remember meeting Matthias Paulsen?"

"The old guy?" Colin asked. "He didn't like us."

"It's not a matter of like. Matthias has been with the Society for ... well, it might as well be forever. Anyway, he gave me the gift—he also gave it to Sarah."

"That's two," Lisa said. "He no longer has his gift?"

"He was old when I first came into the CS and already having trouble getting to people fast enough," Archer said. "The thing is, I can't tell my story without telling you hers. But it's not a secret. You see, Sarah was married to an excellent man named Jacob Pickett."

"Was he part of the CS?" Lisa asked.

"No. At the time, neither of them knew about the CS. Matthias just happened to live next door to them. I was Matthias's apprentice, so I was at his house all the time." Archer flashed a quick smile. "Sarah and Jacob were more like family to Matthias. They even had a weekly cribbage night that I tried to avoid."

"Cribbage?" Colin wrinkled his nose. "My crazy grandpa makes me play when we visit."

"Not a fan myself, but to cut to the chase, Matthias had a vision of Jacob's death."

Lisa let out a small gasp, Colin peered down at his hands, and I knew where this story was going now.

Glancing at Lisa, Archer said, "You know how it goes sometimes. This wasn't a win. Afterward, Matthias blamed himself. He decided he was too old. He gifted me visions, thinking I would have done better to notice more from the vision that might have made a difference. After Jacob's funeral, Sarah thanked us. She'd figured out we'd tried to save him. So Matthias told her everything—without the permission of the CS." He shook his head. "So you see, we all have our own ways of handling things. Sarah joined up, and Matthias gave her the gift right away. I have a feeling if he had waited, he might not have been able to find the nerve to do that. It's hard to give your visions away."

I stared at the empty peanut bag in my hand. Would I gift my visions to someone else? Would I want them going through what I did? Or would I want to give this up now? Even with bad days, like at the hot springs, I'd saved more than I'd lost. A weight lifted off my chest. I imagined a scoreboard, with me versus Death, and I was in the lead. If I kept that lead, I could feel good about what I did. I'd know I was making a difference.

My stomach growled, and I actually felt like I could eat something more than peanuts. If Archer and guys like Matthias had fails, where they'd lost close friends, then anything could happen. And there was just zero chance I'd save everyone. *Zero.* I glanced at Colin, who was watching the crowd. I should be more like him. I could look at this like it was *Halo* or some other game. Or a competition. Us versus Death.

We could do this.

I saw another plane taking off for part of the show. McKnight would have been flying about now, but we had stopped that, so I smiled.

That's when the visions hit.

CHAPTER 16

Color drained out of the sky, out of the people around me, out of the trees and the grandstands. I sat frozen, unable to move. McKnight sat on the grandstand railing, but I knew he wasn't really there. This was just a vision of him. Same as before, I watched his arms and legs tear back in impossible ways. His uniform caught fire. His face burned away. He opened his mouth, and a scream came out. He vanished, but the next vision hit right away.

Around me, people seemed to turn and stare, but they weren't really here, at least not the things I was looking at. These were vision people. Mouths opened wide, they screamed. The sound hit me in a raw wave. I wanted to slap my hands over my ears, but I couldn't even blink. I stared as the world all around me caught fire. I'd never seen a vision play out with this kind of clarity. It had always been just people, but not this time. Flames licked toward the people in the vision. The grandstand pillars collapsed in giant piles of concrete. Clouds of dust dimmed the sunlight and even though I knew what I was seeing wasn't real, I shielded my eyes. Pale gray people caught fire. Their bodies twisted. Other bodies flew apart. The flames licked up, and the screams turned from terror into something worse. I watched them burn, their skin turn black and fall off, and their clothes flame out.

The vision cut off and left me gasping for air.

I braced myself just in case another one was going to start, but the world around me came back into color and I knew it was over.

My stomach twisted, and I almost lost the peanuts I'd eaten. I felt Colin's hand on my shoulder, and Lisa was standing next to where Archer sat. He looked like I felt— pale, shaken, about ready to pass out. He was hunched over, his eyes closed. I didn't want to shut mine in case I saw those burning faces again.

Wetting my lips, I managed to choke out, "I saw about fifty people. And McKnight again. I saw him first. But there were CS members in there too, Archer. I saw them. It's a new vision, isn't it? We didn't stop the accident. We just changed when it will happen."

Hands shaking, Archer pulled out his phone. "Start your countdowns," he said, keeping his voice even and calm.

I don't know how he did that. My hands quaked so hard Colin had to take my phone from me and set my countdown. He didn't say anything about it, so I didn't mention it either.

"Archer," I began, "that was different. I saw more

than just the people. I saw the grandstands; I saw fire and debris ..."

He nodded. "Me too. I've heard of others seeing it like that too. I think it has to do with the number of victims. Like I said before, it's like the vibration that we tune into. Perhaps when there are enough vibrations the vision clarifies. Makes it easier to know exactly what's going to happen." He shook his head and turned back to his phone.

Lisa turned away from Archer and scanned the crowd. "It was so weird watching you guys. You could tell who's CS—they all stopped. Whatever they were doing, they stopped and stood still ... except for a few who crouched."

Colin stood beside her. "Not everyone. We obviously don't get the visions, but we—you and I kept moving. So did Nathan. I saw him watching Dean. It's weird how he's almost tracking you. It was like he was timing you. And speak of the devil ..." Colin halted his words as Nathan walked over to us.

Nathan didn't hesitate. "What did you see?"

He seemed upset, angry almost. But he also sounded like he couldn't hold back the question or his curiosity. Was that because he didn't have visions or because we hadn't stopped the accident? I didn't know, and I had other things to think about.

Trying to remember every detail, I started telling them

what I'd seen about McKnight and the people dying. I had to force myself to replay the vision, but I knew the details mattered. Archer stared at his phone as I spoke.

When I finished, he said, "I'm getting reports from everyone. We all had that vision."

"Not everyone," Nathan muttered. He wouldn't meet Archer's stare.

"Why do you keep watching Dean, Nathan?" Colin asked. "I've seen fanboys before, but aren't you a little old for that?"

Nathan stared at him for a minute, but then the corner of his mouth lifted. "In case you hadn't noticed, Dean is the key to this. He is the only one who saw McKnight."

"Not today." Archer pushed to his feet. "I saw that too. I made it a point to meet McKnight yesterday. A lot of us did."

Nathan's eyebrows lifted. "Really?"

"Yeah, so why all the interest in Dean?" Colin asked. He folded his arms and tipped his head to one side.

"There is one advantage to not having the gift," Nathan explained. "If you're on the outside, you can observe the visions. You can time them, just like I did with Dean. Did you know, the average vision lasts only thirty seconds? This one went on for ninety. Most people don't really handle their visions all that well. I've seen people freeze up for hours after one. Just sitting there, or standing, unable to process what they've seen. Others just lose control."

I winced. I'd done both.

Nathan kept on. "Being part of the CS means you need to prepare yourself to have those visions. Dean got his gift by accident. I'll be fully prepared when I get the gift." He turned away from Colin and went straight to Archer. "They're going to want us back at HQ to regroup. I'm heading back now. Sarah and Hank are going to want to pull in everyone from this and every other nearby district."

As he strode away, Colin shook himself. "That is one weird guy. Prepared for visions? How do you get ready to see people die?"

Lisa nodded in agreement. "I couldn't do it. I don't think it's that great a gift."

"It isn't for everyone," Archer explained. "That's why the CS tries to be careful who does get the gift. And I'm not sure Nathan will ever be ready. This isn't something you really can prepare for."

"Tell me about it," I mumbled.

We followed Archer to his car. Like Nathan had said, Sarah called everyone to the CS headquarters to regroup and meet again. We spent two hours comparing visions and trying to identify all the faces we'd seen. Doris started printing out photos of every person identified.

Her skills using social media and the internet must've rivaled spy agencies'. Sarah sent CS members out to those people to see if we could keep them away from the air show tomorrow.

When Lisa pushed a box of Chinese noodles in front of me, I realized I hadn't had lunch. "It's not bad," she said.

Colin slid in on the other side and handed me a soda. "We went over to the takeout next door. Not much for us to do now. But it's going to be all hands at the air show again tomorrow. My folks are going to start to think I want to become a pilot."

"That's not a bad cover," I said. I started to take a long sip of the soda, but I saw Nathan watching me from the doorway of the CS conference room. He smiled and left. I picked up the Chinese food and a plastic fork.

Before I could bite in, Lisa said, "Okay, you were right." Noodles halfway to my mouth, I saw Lisa nod at Colin. "Nathan is watching Dean a little too carefully and too much."

Colin straightened in his chair. "I told you! There's something wrong."

"With McKnight's plane?" Archer asked, coming over to sit with us. "Yeah, everyone thinks that, too. But I only know one way to find the truth. You guys doing anything tonight?"

I finished my mouthful of noodles and wiped my

mouth. "Why?"

Archer waggled his eyebrow in a sinister manner. "I can't think of anybody better at sneaking into places than you three. So we're going to the air show after it's closed."

CHAPTER 17

Colin cursed when he snagged his jacket on the top wire of the fence. He wiggled free and hit the ground next to me. "Didn't I hear Sarah say it was Nathan's job to make sure McKnight's plane was okay?" he muttered. "Wasn't Nathan bragging about how he knew everything relating to planes?"

Lisa shushed him.

I whispered to Colin, "I think I want a second set of eyes on McKnight's plane too."

Archer came over the fence. We headed to McKnight's hangar. Paul waited for us at the door. He motioned us inside and shut the door after us. "I managed to send the other guys out to get a pizza. Do you have the specs for the plane? We've got about an hour before they come back."

"An hour!" I stared at Paul and swallowed.

"It'll have to be enough," Archer said. He divided the plane into quarters—we'd each take part of it. Paul would go from section to section with each of us, double-checking our checks. In less than an hour, I knew more about the F-86 than I ever wanted to know. Where the fuel tanks sat, how the engine worked, where to find the lines that controlled the flaps and rudders to steer the plane. Colin got to sit in the pilot's seat to check the gauges, and a jab of envy shot through me. But I got to poke my head up into where the wheels lifted up into the belly of the plane. Lisa went through the checklist like she was in charge.

Then she looked at her watch and called out, "That's it. We have to go. And we're done."

Colin looked up, a smear of grease on his cheek. "But we haven't found anything."

Paul shook his head. "You're not going to. I've been over this plane so many times I'm sick of looking at it."

"Did Nathan find anything?" Lisa asked.

Paul glanced at her. "He was here once. Frankly, he didn't seem that interested. He just poked into the pilot's cockpit."

"So much for Mr. I-Know-Everything-About-Planes," Colin muttered to me.

A voice outside drifted to us, someone laughing and joking. Paul waved for us to follow him. "That's the other guys. Quick. Out the back."

He hurried us to a side door. Stepping into the cool night, I shivered. We waited until all the other members of McKnight's flight crew had stepped inside. Archer went first, and we headed back to the fence. Archer boosted

Lisa over first, then Colin, and then me. He climbed over the fence and jumped onto the grass next to us.

"What now?" I asked.

Archer sucked in a breath. "We're coming up on the last day of the air show. If we can make it through tomorrow, we'll be okay."

One more day, I thought. But I hated Archer calling it the "last" day.

I got home and found Becky sitting up, waiting for me. She sat cross-legged on my bed. I gave a small groan. "Oh, look, it's the tooth fairy."

She narrowed her eyes. "I could tell Mom and Dad you were out all night and snuck into the house!"

Too tired to fight, I flopped onto my bed and kicked off my shoes. I hooked my phone into the wall charger. Somehow Becky tattling on me didn't rank up there with what I'd been through today. Maybe getting grounded would be the best thing that could happen to me.

"Go ahead," I told her and gave a wave. I closed my eyes, but I kept seeing the vision over and over.

Something thunked onto my chest. "Some cultures think it's good luck."

Sitting up, I opened my eyes. I pulled back. "It's a tooth!"

"It's a shark tooth. A fossilized shark tooth." Becky pushed off from the bed. "It's the best one I have, so don't lose it."

"You don't believe in luck."

"Of course not. But if *you* think things will work out well, you're more likely to get a positive outcome."

I fingered the sharp edges. When I looked up, Becky had already left. I put the tooth in my pocket. I didn't know if it would bring me any luck, but I was ready to take all the help I could get.

And I knew that I would need it when I walked into the kitchen the next morning and saw Mom packing a picnic lunch.

Her smile dropped when she saw me wearing the same clothes from yesterday, but she said, "I thought we could all go to the air show. It's the last day to see the stunt pilots, and there's supposed to be a special performance by an Australian pilot."

No. Oh, no.

No way could my parents or Becky come to the air show. *Think fast, Dean.* What could I say? There's a flu going around and they might get sick? Too weak. Bomb threat? Too strong. Besides, how would I know that? Becky—I could use Becky. I hurried to her room and caught her just coming out. She gave me a weird look, but I caught her by the shoulders.

"You know how you owe me for that car thing?"

"Uh-huh." She nodded and kept looking at me

sideways.

"Well, I'm calling in the favor. Right now. We can't let Mom and Dad go the air show today." She opened her mouth, but I held up a finger. "No, don't ask. Just ... be sick or something. Like a really-keep-Mom-home kind of sick and Dad won't go without her. Can you do that? Please, Becky. Please."

Her eyes glossed like tears were coming. "Tell me what's going on, Dean."

I pointed at her. "Do this, and we're even. You don't owe me anything. Nothing. I won't even say anything about your frizzy hair anymore."

"Are you staying home?" she asked.

I didn't answer.

"You stay too, and I'll do it."

"I can't, Becky."

"Please, Dean. Whatever you're doing, stop. Just don't do it. Whatever you're involved in, stop being involved in it."

"Today's the last day, Becky. Do this, and not only are we even, I'll owe you."

We stared at each other for a few seconds. She must've seen the desperation on my face or heard it in my voice because she agreed and added, "Two weeks of your allowance, and you help me tag the rest of my teeth tomorrow."

"Done," I said without even thinking about it.

"Please be safe, Dean," she whispered as she stepped out of the room. A few seconds later I heard her wail, "Moooom!"

I didn't think it would work, but when I got there, Mom had the temperature reading strips out, Dad was holding Becky and rocking her, and my sister was whimpering. Mom looked up at me. "Oh, Dean, I'm so sorry. I think your sister is getting the flu. It's been going around. We're going to have to miss the air show."

"Oh, no problem." I gave a shrug like it didn't matter. But I let out a long, quiet breath.

Over the top of Becky's frizzy hair, Dad looked at me. "I'll get Becky to bed, and you and I could—"

"Daaaddy!" Becky curled her arms around his neck. "I think I'm going to be sick."

He got up and carried her to the bathroom. Looking frazzled, Mom leaned against the kitchen counter. I felt bad leaving them like this with Becky, so I said, "Hey, maybe we can just do a picnic when Becky's feeling better?"

Mom gave me a smile. I told her I was heading out to hang out with Colin and Lisa, and I left before they could start thinking I needed them to keep me company with anything. A block away from my house, Nathan pulled up in front of me in a Mustang. He reached over and opened the passenger door. "Get in."

"Uh, I—"

"Don't be such a wimp. I told Archer I'd pick you up. He's getting your friends."

"Oh," I said, and climbed in.

Nathan had on a black windbreaker, a black T-shirt, and black jeans. Except for the sunglasses, he didn't look ready for a hot summer day. He kept his eyes on the road and drove with one hand on the wheel and the other in his coat pocket. "It's going to be a big day."

I pulled out my CS phone and fiddled with it. "You sound like you're looking forward to it."

He smiled. "Hey, everyone from six districts of the CS will be there. Sarah pulled even more people in. Should be interesting, eh?"

"Interesting? Not exactly a word I'd use," I said.

Nathan gave a laugh. He drove faster than Archer and parked a long way away from the grandstands. "Just in case we don't stop things," he said. "Don't want to lose my ride, now do I?" He smiled like all of this was funny.

The back of my neck kept tingling. I put my phone back into my jeans pocket.

Nathan started walking toward the grandstand. I tucked two fingers into my pockets and trailed after him. I couldn't think of anything to say, so I told him about having to keep my parents home today.

"You're lucky to still have your folks." He sounded like he really meant it, and I remembered Archer saying

Nathan's dad had been in the CS and had died before he could pass on his gift. I didn't know if I should say anything, but Nathan stopped and faced me. "Did Archer tell you my dad was in the CS?"

I nodded. "He didn't say much more."

Nathan pulled off his sunglasses. "Yeah, he wouldn't. He doesn't like to tell stories that aren't his own. My dad—he had the gift. For a long time, I thought I'd get it from him. He told me if I still wanted it, when I was old enough, he'd gift me visions. But then he got sent to prison." Nathan glanced at me, the corner of his mouth lifting in a crooked smile. "They arrested him for causing someone's death—a death he'd tried to stop. But he wouldn't say anything about the CS."

"Couldn't the CS get him out or something? Get a lawyer for him?"

"Oh, they did. They had all kinds of people working on his case when he was knifed in a prison riot. He was still trying to stop someone from dying—another prisoner. I was just a little older than you at the time."

He started walking toward the grandstands. I hurried to catch up. I stuffed my hands back into my pockets and just about cut my finger on Becky's shark tooth. I touched the tooth and thought about Becky and my folks. What would I do if my dad died like that?

"Nothing like that should ever happen to anyone in

the CS," Nathan said, his voice flat. "If people knew about the CS, my dad would never have been accused of anything. He'd be around still. He'd be saving people. And we'd all be heroes."

His voice changed. It had gone low and hard, like he would never be able to forget about what had happened to his father.

I reached out and touched his shoulder. "I'm sorry, man. I can't even imagine what that must've been like."

He looked at me and said, "Someday we'll fix it— won't we? We'll make the world see who we really are. Come on. Let's go see what McKnight's doing."

Nathan knew his way around the fairgrounds better than me. He took a shortcut past the food trucks to the hangars that had been set up behind the grandstands. Smells from the food trucks left my mouth watering, and my stomach growled. I hadn't been able to eat breakfast, and I was sure I wouldn't be able to get anything down now. But hot dogs and chicken skewers smelled really good.

"Cool shortcut," I said. "You really know your way around the place."

Nathan smiled. "Never rely on just what the CS tells you. Doris is a know-it-all, but she's like the rest of them— holding stuff back just so she can feel like she's better than you. Always do your own research. And always scope out the area you have to work in."

I'd only met Doris a couple of times, but that didn't sound like her. Archer had said Nathan was smart, and now I began to wonder just how smart. It was a good idea to have been all over the fairgrounds before this.

We'd made it to McKnight's hangar. A bunch of people stood outside, and the hangar doors stood open. I could see McKnight's plane and his flight crew checking it out. McKnight stood outside the hangar with his wife, Sophia. His daughter, Maddie, bounced around, her walkie-talkie in hand. The CS wouldn't be able to distract McKnight today with any kind of fake family emergencies.

Then I saw Rylee standing over to the side, taking a photo of McKnight. My stomach dropped. She might not want to see me, but I had to figure out a way to get her out of here. Leaving Nathan, I walked over to Rylee. "Hi."

She glanced at me and put her cell phone back into her shoulder purse. "Hi. I didn't think you'd be here today." There was a coldness in her tone—like she was trying to show me she wasn't into me the way she'd been before. I couldn't tell if it was an act or if she really wasn't into me anymore. But I was surprised by how okay I was with that. She pushed her hair back. She had on another sundress, something short and white, and she looked really cute. I wanted her to go on looking that way, but she wouldn't if she stayed here.

"Last day of the air show—where else would I be?" I said.

Fiddling with her purse strap, she nodded, and a small smile crossed her face. "Well, if you want, not that it's a big deal, but maybe we could hang out together?"

I thought about that. Would I be able to look after Rylee better if I had her with me? However, what if more visions hit me? I couldn't let her see that. And I didn't even know if I was safe here today. I had to get rid of her, and I knew only one way to do that. After this, Rylee would probably never talk to me again, but at least she'd be out of danger today.

I blew out a breath and hoped I didn't over- or undersell what I was about to do. I adopted a tone I'd heard Eric use a hundred times. "Nah, I don't think that's a good idea, Rylee." I scratched the back of my head and tried really hard to sound completely indifferent. "If we hang out, people might think we're together and"—I laughed—"I don't think we want *anyone* thinking that."

She shook her head, and her eyes got all glossy. "We don't?"

I laughed. "You and me? No way."

"Yeah, I guess you're right." She stared at me with sad eyes. "Is that why you didn't want me to come here? Because you thought I'd bother you?"

My throat caught. *This is for the greater good, Dean*, I

told myself. I couldn't speak, so I just shrugged and made a face that I hoped said, "Sorry."

"Well, I was just leaving anyway," she said. "Sorry if I bothered you before. I won't anymore. I promise."

I pointed to the closest exit. "I think there's a bus stop just outside those gates."

"I'm surprised you and Eric aren't better friends," she said, and her voice caught. "You two are more alike than I thought." Her lower lip trembled.

I wanted to take it all back. I liked her, but if she stayed, and something happened to her ... I folded my arms and shrugged again.

She turned and strode away, almost running from me.

I stood with my arms folded, feeling like the biggest jerk on the entire planet.

From behind me, I heard Colin say, "Kinda harsh, Dean."

"What he said," Lisa echoed.

Colin had dressed a lot like Nathan, in black jeans and a black T-shirt but without the windbreaker. He seemed hot and sweaty. Lisa had on shorts and a T-shirt as well as her running shoes. With her hair pulled back, she looked ready for a track meet. Or a lot of action.

Lisa's mouth twisted down. "What do you think you're doing?"

"Saving lives," I said.

Colin swapped a worried stare with Lisa and said, "Dean, you need to lighten up."

"And you need to remember the more people we send home, the less dead bodies we'll have around here." I looked away, my face hot.

I heard Archer's voice next to Colin. "Hey, guys. You ready for the day?"

"Oh, yeah. Dean's about ready to have a breakdown of some kind, I have knots on the knots in my stomach, and Lisa's chewed off half of her fingernails so far," Colin said.

"I have not," Lisa muttered.

Archer didn't seem to even notice. He was looking around the air show grounds. It already seemed more crowded than any other day. The show started earlier today because it also ended early. I had checked on the program, and a special time had been cleared for McKnight's flight. After the delays, McKnight was the star today.

"Keep it together, guys," Archer said. "We're going to have our hands full today. Sarah's done everything she could, but Hank keeps telling her she can't send everyone from the CS here." He sounded almost as frustrated as Nathan. Archer scrubbed a hand through his hair. He gave us a tight smile. "We really do need to shake things up in the CS. I'm half tempted to call in a bomb threat to the air show just to clear this place today and make it safe. But if I do, it'll be my last act in the CS. Hank would flip out. And

I'd probably be tracked by Homeland Security and jailed for the next few years."

I glanced around at the crowd, the back of my neck still tingling. Something from one of my visions kept nagging at me. Not something I had seen, but something I'd missed seeing. "There's got to be another way," I said, talking more to myself than anyone. "Change ..." I noted.

Something had changed between the two different visions I had. Not the visions of McKnight, but the visions of the other people in the grandstand.

What was it?

CHAPTER 18

Colin and Lisa kept staring at me like I really had lost it, but I felt like I was close to figuring out this puzzle. The heat of the day closed around me. The long days had left me tired and not really thinking straight. But I knew whatever was bugging me had something to do with what Nathan had been saying. He'd talked about change, just like Archer. However, Archer had sounded frustrated. Nathan sounded certain, more like the CS had already changed.

"Dean!" I saw Nathan headed toward us, hands tucked into his windbreaker even though the sun beat down hot enough to leave my underarms damp. Colin gave a groan, and even Lisa shifted on her feet like she didn't know how to act around Nathan anymore.

"Archer," Nathan said with a nod. "Mind if I take Dean with me for another patrol of the grounds?"

Archer deferred to me. "It's Dean's choice."

I checked my watch; we had just under forty minutes left. I started to tell Nathan I wanted to stay close to McKnight. The pilot had his plane out of the hangar and looked like he was checking it over before his flight.

Nathan grabbed my arm. "Come on, Dean. Let's see if we can get security to close the grandstands. Maybe tell them the fire marshal wants it closed so it's not too crowded."

"Wouldn't you need documentation for that?" I asked. He didn't answer. He just dragged me with him; I didn't really see how I couldn't go. He kept hold of my arm. Instead of heading for the grandstands, Nathan strode toward the main gates.

"Is this a shortcut?" I asked. "I thought you wanted to close the grandstands."

Nathan didn't let go of me. He didn't answer, either. I started wishing I had Colin and Lisa close. Or Archer. Or anyone. I tried to hold back, to drag my feet, but Nathan tightened his hold on my arm and kept pulling. I thought about the martial arts he knew. If I tried anything, he could flatten me and then still drag me with him.

What was going on?

He stopped a short distance away from the main gates in one of the aisles of parked cars. The sunlight bounced off windshields and blacktop. An old guy who took tickets sat on a stool at the gates, an umbrella over him. Two security guards leaned on the fence, watching the street traffic pass by, their security carts—golf carts really—sitting nearby. I thought about calling out to them, but Nathan had stopped us far enough away that I wasn't sure they'd hear me. Overhead, but close to the ground, planes roared. I heard the crowd in the grandstand yelling and clapping.

Nathan twirled his sunglasses in one hand. "You're going to be a hero today."

I jerked away from him, and he let go. "Y'know, we learned in school that the Greeks who started all this hero stuff said a guy had to be dead before they called him that."

Nathan's mouth quirked at the corner. "That's why I like you. You've got nerve, Dean. You're not afraid to tell people what you think. But you *are* going to be a hero. After Vidmar died, I thought, well ... I knew no one else at the CS would gift me visions." He shook his head. "And then before he died the old coot gives *you* the gift. Worst day of my life. I thought I'd never get what I wanted, but now it's all going to work out."

Worst day? Worse than his father dying? Nathan was officially freaking me out.

He clapped a hand on my shoulder. "After today, we'll remake the CS, you and I. We'll do it together. All this secrecy crap that's holding us back, we'll dump it. We'll tell people what happened here. It'll be great. Archer's been right all along about the CS needing to figure out how to do things better. His problem was not going far enough."

"But you will?" I backed up another step and bumped into a truck that was parked right near where we stood.

"Nathan, how far are you going?"

He grinned wickedly, his hands still inside the windbreaker pockets. Sweat glistened on his forehead. "We're both headed to the top. You're just what the CS needs. Archer was right about that. Young, gifted. I can mold you into the right kind of visionary for the CS. We'll get rid of this zone and district stuff—it's a useless structure. Outdated. The CS needs someone who'll run it right. Who'll take charge."

Nathan withdrew a silver box from his pocket. He ran his thumb over the edge, and I glimpsed a joystick. Sunlight glinted off the box and flashed in my eyes, almost as blinding as a vision.

I sucked in a hard breath when I realized what I hadn't seen in that second vision of the deaths in the grandstands.

I'd seen faces of CS members—a lot of them. But I hadn't seen Nathan.

He wasn't going to die today. That's why he wanted to be standing here, as far from the grandstands as possible. And that meant he knew what was going to happen and was ready for it. I could think of only one reason why he'd know all that. He didn't have the visions, so he had to know about it because he had something to do with it.

I looked over to the woods on our right, where McKnight was due to fly overhead. Even from here, I could hear the birds squawking. The last piece clicked into place.

My mouth fell open, and I forced the words out.

"You're planning a bird strike on McKnight's plane."

Nathan laughed. "Birds? Good one. Like I'd rely on them." He held up the box in his hand. "The birds are a distraction. *Maybe* the birds hit the plane, maybe they don't. But I don't rely on maybes, Dean." He gave the remote a shake. "Do you know how inexpensive drones are these days? Honestly. I picked this one up for a couple grand. I threw a tracker on McKnight's plane the other day and an IED in the drone, and presto." He smiled a creepy, psychotic smirk and dipped his head in a kind of bow. "McKnight's going to be blamed for the whole thing. Good, isn't it? The drone has feathers on it. A tragic end, I'm afraid, but the CS will be thrust into the spotlight, and those of us who remain will see to it that it's reborn ... like a phoenix from the ashes."

Sweat clung to my back and dripped down my forehead. Nathan was completely nuts. But it still didn't explain how he was going to kill everyone. Maybe it was possible that McKnight would crash into the grandstands, but there was no way that was guaranteed. We weren't *that* close. Odds were he'd crash into a field, or maybe not even crash at all.

No, Nathan had a plan—he was too confident, and as crazy as he was, he was smart. I remembered my dad telling me that sometimes the best thing a therapist could do to make one of their patients talk was to say nothing.

So that's what I did.

Nathan kept right on talking, seemingly convinced I was on team crazy along with him.

"I'll be the highest ranking CS member left in this entire area," he said. "There's going to be at least six districts left without leaders, if all goes well. But you can gift me visions, Dean—or I can get one of the dying CS members to gift them to me. Either way works. We'll expand. Going public will put me in control of the entire West Coast. Plus, once I step out into the limelight, I'll become the face of the Society. The others will fade away. You'll be my right-hand man. Think of it, Dean. Punks like those two jerks I got rid of for you the other day will worship you."

I thought about how Nathan had used his martial arts skills on Eric and Rodney. My mouth dried like an arid desert. Nathan was talking about killing way more than fifty people today. And he made it sound like nothing to him. I didn't know his whole plan, but I knew I had to stop him. I just didn't know how.

"Hey, Dean," Colin called out.

Nathan and I both spun around.

Colin and Lisa wove their way between the rows of parked cars, headed for us. "Archer needs help clearing the grandstands. Sarah's given the CS the order to do that, and they're about to start. We need everyone over there."

Nathan's mouth tightened. I didn't trust him not to hurt Colin and Lisa. If he'd take out the CS, he wouldn't think twice about hurting my friends.

Clutching my head, I staggered. I shifted my stare to the right, to an empty point in space like I was seeing something, and I gave a groan.

Lisa hurried over to me. "Dean—is it a vision?"

It felt like forever, but I tried to wait about thirty seconds before I brought myself out of my fake vision and looked straight at Nathan. I didn't know how to make my skin go pale, but I thought about all the deaths he planned, and my stomach flipped in disgust. I was pretty sure that helped me look like I'd just seen something bad.

"It's your death," I told Nathan. "You're going to die."

CHAPTER 19

Nathan lunged toward me, his mouth tight. He shook his head like he didn't really believe me, but he asked, "What did you see?"

I put a hand to my skull and looked down as if I was dizzy. Angling my head, I winked at Colin and Lisa, so Nathan wouldn't see. Colin stiffened, picking up on my message. Lisa moved closer to Nathan.

"What'd you see?" Nathan asked again, almost shouting at me.

I played it up to the hilt. "You're mangled. Twisted up worse than I've ever seen. Maybe a car wreck? Maybe just hit by a car. I thought I caught a glimpse of *silver* ... maybe it was part of the car. I'm not sure but it's important. It's dangerous, whatever it was."

I didn't know if Lisa or Colin would get that keyword. My visions were black and white, and something silver would probably look about the same in color or in gray scale, but I hoped they'd get the message. I hoped I wasn't being too obvious and that it wouldn't click for Nathan since it pretty much gave away the fact that I was faking it.

He lifted his hand like he wanted to grab and shake me. The silver box in his hand reflected a burst of sunlight. Realization flashed in Lisa's eyes, and she lunged out and grabbed Nathan's wrist. I'd seen her make the same move when Nathan was showing her how to use martial arts. She turned and twisted his arm up over her head. He gave a shout, but Lisa had him off balance. She threw him over her hip. His head hit the side mirror of a truck, hard, and he fell to the ground. He lay there, groaning. The silver box flew out of his hand and flashed in the air.

Lisa stepped back. "Is he—?"

"Grab it," I yelled to Colin. We both lunged for the box, but it sailed over our heads, smacked into the bumper of the same truck Nathan had hit, and then clattered onto the pavement.

I grabbed it.

Too late.

The whine of an engine started. I looked over at the woods and saw something metal lift up into the air. "It's a drone," I shouted. "Nathan planned to fly it into McKnight's plane."

Grabbing for the remote, Lisa worked at the controls. Buttons were missing, and there was a toggle that was totally busted. "I think it's broken."

Overhead, we heard a jet engine. "Look!" Colin shouted. He pointed to the sky. "That's McKnight's F-86."

Lying on the ground, Nathan groaned. I shaded my eyes, trying to see the drone. Birds scattered up from the woods. I saw sunlight reflect off metal. It looked like the drone was spooking the birds, keeping them in the air.

"Lisa, see if you can crash that thing. Colin, come on. We have to get everyone out of the grandstands."

"I've got a better plan," Lisa said. She took off at a run with the drone remote control. I was going to shout at her to tell me what she was doing, but there wasn't time. I had to trust her. I did trust her.

Behind me, I heard Nathan moaning again. He started to sit up and fell back, clutching his head. Then he threw up. Blood dripped down the back of his neck.

A twinge of pity for him shook me, but he'd gotten himself into this. He gave a laugh and said, "You can't change what's meant to be. Maybe you'll save McKnight, but he was a distraction. He'd be blamed, that's it. You two are idiots. You can't stop the explosion."

Head swimming, I looked at Colin. He stared back. "What explosion?" he asked.

I lifted my hands, and Colin's head shot up. Nathan's gaze shifted for just a second—totally involuntary—and I followed the gaze until I saw what he'd done.

"The trucks!" I blurted. "It has to be the fuel trucks. They're close enough to the grandstands. He put an explosive on the drone, and if he put another one on the trucks—"

Colin jabbed a finger toward the fuel trucks. I imagined if McKnight's plane went down, and then, shortly after, the two trucks exploded, people would think they'd been struck by shrapnel. They very well could be. Nathan just took chance out of the equation. He'd rigged them. I was sure of it. They were definitely going to explode.

Nathan gave another barking laugh. "Go ahead, be heroes," he said. He started to push up to his feet, but Colin spun and kicked him, hard, and Nathan sprawled on the ground, unmoving, and Colin dusted his hands. "That's for when you dropped me on my butt."

I grabbed Colin's arm, and we started for the fuel trucks. "Come on, we don't have time."

"No, wait," Colin said. He pulled me the other way, toward the main gate. Was he thinking of leaving? I couldn't believe it. But Colin slipped into one of the security carts. "My dad uses these on the studio lots all the time," he said.

I glanced at the security guards. They were talking to a vendor who'd come by to sell them cold drinks. They hadn't even noticed our scuffle with Nathan. Colin flipped a switch, and the cart took off with a quiet hum. I launched myself into the seat next to Colin.

"Electric. Sweet ride," Colin said.

We took off. Two seconds later, the guards shouted,

and I glanced back to see them scrambling for the other security cart. "Punch it," I ordered.

Colin did, and the cart shot forward.

I glanced up and saw the birds still in the air—a huge flock of them. The drone flying around with them must've somehow kept them scared. Suddenly, the drone took a nosedive. It crashed into a tree with a crack, and although that took care of the drone, the crash launched even more birds into the sky.

"Lisa?" Colin asked.

"I hope so," I said. Colin wove in and out of the parked cars and headed for the fuel trucks. The guards missed a turn and hit a car. They backed up and started for us again. "Hurry."

"Going as fast as we can. These things aren't Indy 500–ready," Colin said.

Even so, the wind bit into our faces. I leaned out, but I couldn't see McKnight's plane. I could hear the drone of his jet's engine. "Where is he?" I asked. And then I saw the silver of his jet, turning and heading to fly over the woods.

We reached the trucks and Colin skidded to a stop so fast that it flung me out of the cart. I rolled and shot back up to my feet. My elbows burned from losing skin, but I shouted out at Colin. "Two fuel trucks. Two of us," I ordered. Colin climbed into one while I struggled up into the other and stared at all the controls. There were buttons and levers and dials. I didn't know where to start.

"How do you start these?" I yelled out.

Colin smacked a lever by the wheel. "Ignore everything but this, just put it in gear and step on the gas." He dangled keys from his window. "Keys were in the visor." I checked the visor and found keys as well. I put it in the ignition, turned it, and glanced over my shoulder. McKnight was still headed for the woods and the birds.

The jet pulled up in a sudden, fancy move. He must be dodging birds. But something happened. His engine sputtered and cut off. The silence sent a chill into me. McKnight's plane wobbled and started to fall.

"Gotta go," I muttered and tried to start the engine. It grumbled and died out on me. I stretched my foot for the gas pedal. "Now ... now!" I thought about Becky's shark tooth. Maybe it wasn't such good luck. It certainly hadn't helped the shark. I turned the key again. This time, the engine roared. I heard Colin's truck start as well. I grabbed the shifter and pulled it to the drive position. The truck lurched before I'd even touched the gas. When I did step on the gas pedal I was shocked how fast the huge truck moved. I turned the wheel and drove—anywhere farther away from people would do. The truck jerked forward. I skidded past the guys in the security cart. They spun their wheel and raced out of my way. I steered the truck away from grandstands and people. In my peripheral vision, I saw Colin doing the same. We were off-roading in fuel trucks that literally were going to explode. It was all I could do not to jump out and run screaming for cover.

And then, I saw McKnight's plane coming down. Nathan's plan was working. Despite it all, it was working.

We had to be far enough away by now, but I kept driving. Ten more seconds, I told myself. We were both headed away from the crowd across the grassy part of the airport—across the field right toward the grove of trees and, oh crap! McKnight's plane pitched, and rolled, but in a way that seemed to be aiming for the same area we were headed. Clearly McKnight had seen the area as the safest place to crash, just like we had, and now he was doing what he could to maneuver his plane. If wreckage from his crash didn't hit us, it was going to be close.

That was it.

As far as we could go.

I laid on the horn, hoping Colin would hear it and get out of his truck. I slowed the truck I was driving just enough that I could throw myself out of the cab but kept it aimed for the grove of trees. I hit the ground hard, knocking the wind out of my lungs. Colin must've known what I was trying tell him because, when I staggered to my feet, he was already sprinting away from the trucks—his was almost in the trees.

I mustered all my strength and surged forward. Colin

looked over his shoulder.

"Run!" he screamed.

I looked up just in time to see McKnight's plane nosing toward the ground. Then it somehow leveled, and that's when the first truck exploded. I had no idea how, or what caused it, but I imagined Nathan had rigged it with a timer of some kind.

It was as if a four-hundred-pound linebacker had hit me square in the mid-back. I flew through the air and hit the dirt hard. Colin was beside me, coughing and choking, but we were both alive.

We heard sputtering overhead, and then the aircraft slammed into the ground between us and the grandstands. A wing sheared off and pinwheeled through the air right toward the grandstands. I didn't see it hit because that's when the second fuel truck exploded, and the wave of heat that tore over our backs forced my face into the dirt.

I heard screams and shouts—just like in my vision. I shut my eyes and clutched the shark tooth through my jeans.

"Please ... please ... please ..." I whispered. "Please don't let everyone die."

And then, there was an instant of silence.

The next second, sirens started up, and somehow we found the strength to get onto our feet. Colin's eyes were wide, his face caked in dirt, and scratches covered his arms and neck. McKnight's plane was on its side. The wing had impaled itself into the grandstands, and people were rushing around it—helping people who must've not gotten out before it hit. Fire had started around it. Breathing hard, Colin staggered over to me. And that's when it happened. The red scratches on Colin's face turned gray and the world around me became colorless. There was only one person I'd connected with that I was close enough to help at this point.

"We're not done yet," I yelled at him. "Come on!" I ran for the plane.

CHAPTER 20

The plane burst into flames before we reached it. Black smoke swirled into the air. The stink of melted metal and burning fuel choked me. Beside me, Colin coughed. We hit the plane at the same time as four other guys, these ones wearing overalls. McKnight's team or the team of some other pilot maybe. They were shouting orders to each other.

Something is wrong with all of this, I thought. But I kept going.

Security had forgotten about us. I could see uniformed men and women rushing with us to help. Babies cried, and I could hear the howling of people in pain. Slapping Colin's arm to get him to follow me, I headed for McKnight's plane. The heat hit me like opening an oven door. I pushed forward and could see McKnight struggling to get out of his plane. Fire crews arrived in engines. Guys geared up, jumped out, and pulled ladders from their trucks, and hoses started to spray a foam over everything, smothering the flames. Colin and I had the advantage—we'd been over every inch of McKnight's plane.

I grabbed hold of the wing. Even with most of the flames gone, the metal still burned my hands, but I hauled myself up. It wasn't hard since the plane sat tipped at an angle; the other wing was gone. Colin climbed up after me and pulled out a pocketknife. We reached McKnight, and Colin went to work cutting the pilot free. It wasn't until we were pulling him out of the cockpit that I saw his face: a mixture of black soot and blood, and foam from the firefighter's hoses, that I realized my vision had cleared.

He fought for breath, coughing uncontrollably. I dragged one of his arms over my shoulders while Colin took the other. We staggered with him to the edge of the plane's wing. It was slick and none of us could keep our footing; the three of us tumbled off the wreckage in a heap. We were dragged away a second later to the opposite side of one of the fire trucks, where an ambulance crew immediately secured an oxygen mask over my face. I turned and saw them doing the same to Colin and McKnight. They clearly recognized McKnight as the one in the worst condition because they loaded him onto a stretcher. Blood streaked one of his arms, and there were several blood-soaked areas on his jumpsuit. But he was alive.

"Colin! Dean!" Lisa shouted out.

I saw her wave from the edge of the grandstand. She had hold of Maddie McKnight's hand. The little girl was crying, and Lisa picked her up and held her. Colin and I ran toward her.

"Good job crashing that drone," I told her, coughing out black smoke.

"You can thank Maddie and her walkie-talkie," she said. She kissed Maddie's cheek.

Maddie wiped at her tears. "Daddy?"

"He's going to be okay," Colin told her. He grinned at Maddie and then looked at Lisa. "What about her walkie-talkie?"

"You want to tell, Maddie?" Lisa asked. Maddie shook her head so Lisa continued. "Maddie let me talk to her dad, so I could help him avoid most of the birds. I had a good view of what was happening."

I turned to see Mrs. McKnight kneeling by her husband.

Putting two and two together, I told Lisa, "Seems like *you're* the hero today." She turned red from the compliment. I gestured to McKnight. "I think Maddie might want to see her dad, and I'll bet he wants to see her too."

"Dean! Colin!" Archer's shout caught my attention. He waved at us. "We could use your help, as in now!"

"Go on," Lisa said. "I'll see that Maddie gets to her family."

Colin and I headed for where we could see Archer. It looked like the CS had been able to get a lot of people out of the grandstands. When we reached him, he patted us both on the back. "Good job leaving your phone on to record. We heard everything."

Blinking at the smoke in my eyes, I remembered leaving my phone in my pocket on record, like Archer had said we should. That had given the CS enough time to act. I let out a breath, and Archer said, "It's mostly minor injuries, but let's see what we can do to help."

Everywhere I looked I saw someone in uniform. Fire fighters, police officers, security, and EMTs trying to help people. For a little bit, it seemed like a mess of crying and hurt people, but eventually things were under control. Areas were set up to deal with those who'd been closest to the crash. The burns were the worst. A few bystanders cradled broken arms or lay still with bones sticking out of their legs. That didn't look fun. I saw a guy spread a blanket over someone, covering that person's face, and I turned away. I didn't want to know if I had seen that person in a vision or not.

The only person I'd been close enough to help had been McKnight, and he was alive. I let out a long breath over that.

I heard a girl crying, and there was something familiar in the voice. I turned and saw dark brown hair with sun streaks. Rylee. Heading over to her, I saw she'd gotten stuck in some seats that had been twisted despite being a fair distance from where the wing had actually struck.

"Rylee?" I called out, keeping my voice soft. She stopped crying. "What are you doing here? Are you hurt?"

She shook her head. I held out my hand to her. Eyes big, she reached up and accepted it. I braced one foot against the seat that had her leg pinned, and pushed as hard as I could while pulling her with my arms. It didn't move much, but it was just enough for her to get free. "Let's get someone to look at you."

"I'm fine."

"I don't think anyone's fine today. But I think most of us will be okay. Come on. I think they've set up cold drinks somewhere. I could use a lemonade."

I sat and drank water with her—no lemonade after all—until she seemed to relax her shoulders a bit. "I'm sorry about earlier," I said. "I don't know what came over me. I was ... well, I was a jerk, and I'm sorry about that."

She managed a weak smile and then said her aunt brought her, so I went along to help Rylee find her.

We found her aunt in one of the areas for those who had been hurt, but she wasn't too bad, just a cut across her arm, so the medics wrapped it and told her to go to a hospital to have stitches. I promised to text Rylee tomorrow to see how she was doing and made her promise to go straight home.

Leaving Rylee with her aunt, I started to go, but I saw Eric and Rodney sitting on a bench. Rodney was hunched over, his eyes kind of glazed. Eric looked up, and our stares locked.

Eric's face was wet, and his eyes were red. He glared at me, so I turned away. I wouldn't want Eric to see me crying, either.

I made my way back to Archer. Smoke had darkened his clothes and streaked his face. Lisa and Colin had scored some sodas, and she handed me one.

Archer nodded at me. "Just heard from Sarah. She's okay. But we lost two members today. A total of five dead." Lisa sucked in a breath. Archer reached out to her. "It could have been worse."

"Archer!" We all turned to see Hank Fallston weave his way toward us. Most of those who could go home had left, but a few, like us, sat around, some with blank faces like they couldn't remember who they were. Or maybe they couldn't remember where they'd parked their car. I knew the CS was already working to try and help folks get home.

Hank headed directly at me, and I wondered if he was somehow going to make this my fault.

However, he held out his hand to me. "Good job, Dean. All of you. I was wrong. You not only did your jobs, you did more than anyone could have asked of you."

Colin's mouth hung open while Lisa smiled. I suddenly needed to sit down.

"We're keeping it quiet, but we found the grandstand

pillars had been weakened in key places," Hank said to Archer. "It's why it's so damaged, but it could've been a million times worse if the explosion had happened the way it was supposed to. The entire structure would have collapsed."

Okay, now I did sit down.

Colin looked at me like I was supposed to say something, so I said, "That's why Nathan wanted to stay away from the grandstands and from the fuel trucks. He had a safe spot picked out near the gates."

"And he actually *wanted* all the delays over the past couple days," Hank said with great conviction. "Each intervention we put in place might as well have come right from his plan. The more delayed we were, the more CS members made it. He wanted to take out as much of the CS as he could."

"And he thought Dean was someone he could reshape. Boy, did he get that wrong," Colin said. "Well, are you going to say it?"

"What?" I asked. "The way he was acting was starting to get to me too. But I ... I can't help but feel a little sorry for him. He's probably smart enough to have been running the CS someday without ... Wait. Where is Nathan?" I asked Hank and Archer.

Hank hung his head while Archer said, "Gone. By the time we could send someone to where you left him, we couldn't find a trace of him."

"Oh, that's going to be good," Colin said.

I didn't know if we'd ever see Nathan again. Maybe he would change. Or maybe not. Or perhaps he'd try this stunt someplace else.

"Dean!"

I turned to see my dad waving his hands over his head with my mom in tow. She caught me in a tight hug and just about smothered me. Dad kept his hand on my shoulder as if he was afraid I'd vanish if he let go.

"Colin, Lisa," Dad said, nodding to them, and then he looked toward Archer and Hank. "Dean, you want to introduce your friends?"

"Uh ... they're just some guys who've been helping."

"And who need to find their own families now. Take care," Archer said. He gave me a two-finger salute, and I shivered. That's just what Nathan did. I hoped Archer wouldn't pick up the habit. Hank wandered away from us like he'd never really met us.

"Can we go home?" I asked my parents with an exacerbated breath.

We dropped Lisa off at her place. Her parents ran out to see her inside. At Colin's house, no one came out. But once Colin went inside, I heard Mrs. Blane's voice. "Colin, darling! You're on TV! Come see. You look wonderful!"

The crash was on all the news channels. I got to listen

to it on the radio in the car and then watch it at home as well. It seemed worse on the news, with black smoke billowing and what looked like bits of McKnight's plane spread all over the place.

Mom kept touching my hair and smoothing it, and Dad kept asking if I wanted to talk about it. Becky pulled out her box of teeth and stared ahead, reminding me I'd promised to help her finish tagging them. First, though, Mom made me clean up and eat a bowl of soup—the cure for everything.

Sitting in the living room with Becky, I tried to only tag the animal teeth. But she pushed a human one at me and asked, "Do you think you can get that one signed for me?"

"Me? Why would I be able to get a tooth signed for you?"

She huffed out a breath. "Come on, Dean. Everyone saw you just about save his life! The least he could do is autograph his tooth for you."

I stared at the tooth in her hand. "Is that ..."

"Captain McKnight. The pilot who crashed." She held up the incisor and studied it. "I got it from Dr. Morris."

"Our dentist? How does he know McKnight?"

"He was in Australia last summer for a big dentist conference. McKnight came to see him. Dr. Morris is an expert in tooth implants—he's world famous! Don't you ever listen to anything he talks about when he's cleaning your teeth or filling a cavity?"

I stared at the tooth. Visits to the dentist meant I took everything they would give me to make me not think about drills, especially the headphones and music they offered so you didn't have to hear that noise. The only thing I couldn't avoid was the smell of drilling out the enamel.

Dr. Morris had worked on McKnight. In Australia. And had brought a tooth home, which he had given to Becky. Figured ... Dr. Morris and Becky were both hard-core nerds.

But that totally explained it. I had touched McKnight's tooth. I shivered at the realization, wondering if that meant I could get a vision from any body part.

I promised Becky I'd visit McKnight in the hospital and ask him to sign something for her—but not a tooth. She'd have to settle for getting the label signed.

Before that, I had another promise to keep.

CHAPTER 21

Squinting up at the steps, I shifted from one foot to the other. Colin and Lisa stood beside me outside the museum. Mom had driven us all here, and I had the feeling that if I hadn't asked to come here, Dad would have started dropping hints to me.

The sun beat down on us, baking my head. The back of my T-shirt stuck to my skin. I could have wished us into a movie with large sodas and even larger popcorns, but we had a therapy session coming up. And we had promised Dr. Mickelsen.

"Let's get it done," I said.

Colin frowned like I'd asked him to tear down all his movie posters, and Lisa dragged her feet like she wasn't one of the best runners on the track team at school. We headed inside.

Cool air hit us. Our steps echoed on the floor. The museum had just recently reopened after fixing all the damage we'd caused when we'd been trying to keep a robbery from turning into something worse. Of course, we'd then helped the monks rob the place, but it really was more like returning something that had been stolen from them. That's what I kept telling myself.

We paid the entrance fee and got a guide for the newest exhibit, whatever that was. A couple of security guards started to trail us. Then a couple more.

Colin asked, "Is it just me, or are we being followed?"

"Followed," Lisa said. "You even offer to touch anything, and I'm going to knock you down and sit on your hands."

"She can do it now, too," I said, thinking of how she'd taken down Nathan.

Colin folded his hands behind his back. "Not even thinking it."

We strolled into the first exhibit room. I'd barely turned around when Jonathan Overton, the museum curator, rushed over to us. He stood in front of us, arms crossed and legs spread wide like he wanted to block us from the rest of the museum. A pinched look tightened his mouth like he had sucked on a lemon sour candy for too long.

"Mr. Blane, Mr. Curse, Ms. Green." He gave us each a nod, but he didn't say anything like "nice to see you again" or "how good you've come to improve your minds with a visit."

We all nodded back to Overton.

"You aren't staying long," he said. He made it sound like a fact, not a bit of a question in there.

"Uh ... Dr. Mickelsen said we should come by."

"So he's trying to get rid of you too?"

We swapped looks again. A family came into the room, and Overton smiled at them. He dropped his voice and stepped closer. "A few words of advice. The publicity for the museum is more than I could ever have asked for. We have set new records for visitors, and our donors are happy—for now."

"Uh, we just—"

"Mr. Blane, I am speaking." Overton narrowed his eyes. "You three are like locusts, a plague, a walking invitation to trouble."

Lisa's chin came up. "Locusts are grasshoppers, and a comparison implies we eat everything in sight."

Way to go, Lisa, I thought.

Overton's mouth pinched even tighter. The family left the exhibit room, leaving us with Overton and his security squad. "I don't know everything about your involvement with what happened with our theft a while back, but I do know you were involved. That I don't know to what extent, and that your mother, Mr. Curse, is someone I greatly respect are the only reasons your names were not passed along to the authorities. I forgive you, in essence, only due to the fact that our recovery is better than expected. I will not tempt fate with a second ... incident. I invite you to leave. Now. This offer shall not be repeated."

I nudged Colin and gestured to Lisa. We'd come. We'd seen the place. We could get outta here before an arrest followed.

We trailed out the way we came. Colin couldn't make it to the entrance without some gesture. He touched one of the display cabinets. Alarms went off. Guards started running. We ran, too, and got outside and back into the hot afternoon sun before anything else happened.

I leaned against a tree to catch my breath. I saw Overton standing at the entrance just inside, his arms still crossed. I was pretty sure my museum-visiting days had ended.

A dark head of hair with highlights caught my eye. Turning, I saw Rylee and Rodney heading to the museum. Rylee? With Rodney? They weren't holding hands or anything, but Eric wasn't around. Rylee was talking away to Rodney about something. I couldn't hear what she was saying, but Rodney had this look on his face like Rylee could do anything and he'd think it was the coolest thing since ice cream was invented.

I shook my head.

I wasn't ever going to understand Rylee. But then they'd both just gone through something horrible. Maybe they both needed someone to talk to. Maybe the fact that Rodney hardly spoke made him a good listener.

Colin shoved the exhibit guide at me. I thumbed

through it and read it aloud. "Precious stones from around the world."

"As in diamonds," Colin explained. "Overton probably thought we were casing the place for our next robbery."

"Oh, look, there's Rylee. Hi, Rylee." Lisa waved. Rylee waved back. I slunk back under the tree.

I thought about what Nathan had said—about what had happened to his father. If Nathan had had his way, we would be heroes now. We'd be interviewed. Overton would probably welcome us to his museum and give us a VIP tour or something. The world would be different. So would we.

The CS was outside of everything. We were a secret no one knew about.

Would Rylee still like me if she knew I'd had visions of deaths—and we'd stopped them? Or would she just think I was a freak?

"Do you mind?" I sat on the grass next to Colin. "I mean—us being kicked out?"

Colin pulled at a blade of grass, and Lisa shook her head.

"Nathan didn't believe in sacrifices," I said, and stared up at the sky. Overhead a jet flew by, leaving a white trail. "He thought CS members should be known and ... worshiped."

"Like movie stars. Yuck." Colin tossed away the grass. "Seen that, don't want it. Spies have to be unknown, you know."

I could see a little bit of what Nathan wanted. It'd be a lot easier to just walk up and tell someone, "Don't get on that plane tomorrow," but I thought about the CS name too.

Congregatio de Sacrificio—Congregation of Sacrifice.

A congregation wasn't just a group, but an assembly who held the same beliefs. I'd looked up the word, and it talked about that. That was important. And I could see now why Hank would be worried about someone like me coming into the CS. They tried really hard not to end up with guys like Nathan, but they still had. So, of course, they'd look at me—someone who hadn't been vetted, hadn't been checked out—and wonder if I was bringing them trouble or if I would share their beliefs.

"You look like you're thinking too much," Lisa said, staring down at me.

Pushing off the grass, I brushed off my jeans. "I was thinking we should grab an ice cream and write up our feelings so we have them all ready for therapy this week."

Colin scrambled to his feet. "Yes to the ice cream, no to the feelings."

Lisa pointed her finger. "That reminds me—you owe me an ice cream."

"Do not."

"Do too."

"How do you figure?" Colin asked.

They took off ahead of me, Lisa arguing that Colin had promised her ice cream days ago and Colin pretending to have forgotten. I thought Lisa's walk had a new swagger. She didn't look as beat up about things—meaning she wasn't beating herself up. Colin ... well, Colin was always cool about everything.

I trailed after them, wondering what I would write about my feelings. Maybe something about friends. Or about how giving up one thing doesn't mean you don't get something else in return. Yeah, the visions meant I would miss out on some stuff. But I thought about little Maddie McKnight's face when she'd hugged her dad after he'd gotten out of his crash. I still got warm inside from that.

Lisa called out, "You're slowing us down! Last one to the ice cream parlor buys! And I'm beating both of you in the next game of *Halo*!"

"In your dreams," Colin said.

I nodded. It was all about the dreams and visions, after all.

The End

At fourteen, Matt Cambridge has executed so many pranks – the latest nearly destroying his school – that his parents are out of discipline options. So his father pulls a few questionable strings to get his son into Camp Friendship: A camp that promises to strengthen the moral compass of today's youth. With a name like Camp Friendship Matt imagines three punishing weeks of daisy chains and Kumbayas.

Within minutes of arriving at the camp, however, Matt's nearly killed—twice. It doesn't take long for him to realize there's more to this picture-perfect place than meets the eye. What sort of summer camp has programs in forging passports? Why do they have endless fight training, and weapons drills, and what is with the hidden rooms? Matt wonders if his parents realize they've enrolled him in what seems to be some kind of freakish, elite spy school.

What Matt doesn't yet know – and is soon to find out – is that Camp Friendship's ultimate purpose is far more sinister than he could possibly have imagined. With each dot he connects, he begins to understand that in the end he'll be left with two choices: pull the prank of a lifetime to escape this place ... or die trying.

Learn how Dean's visions all started in...

GLIMPSE, BOOK 1
THE DEAN CURSE CHRONICLES

ISBN 978-0-9919208-0-8 / PB
ISBN 978-0-9919208-2-2 / HC

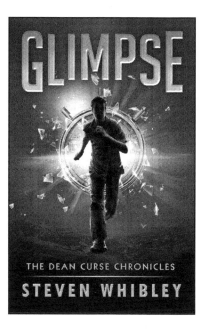

Dean Curse avoids attention the way his best friend Colin avoids common sense. Which is why he isn't happy about being Abbotsford's latest local hero – having saved the life of a stranger, he is now front page news. Dean's reason for avoiding the lime-light? Ever since his heroic act, he's been having terrifying visions of people dying and they're freaking him out so badly his psychologist father just might have him committed. Dean wants nothing more than to lay low and let life get back to normal.

But when Dean's visions start to come true, and people really start dying, he has to race against the clock – literally – to figure out what's happening. Is this power of premonition a curse? Or is Dean gifted with the ability to save people from horrible fates? The answer will be the difference between life and death.

WWW.STEVENWHIBLEY.COM

RELIC, BOOK 2
THE DEAN CURSE CHRONICLES

ISBN 978-0-9919208-4-6 / PB
ISBN 978-0-9919208-5-3 / HC

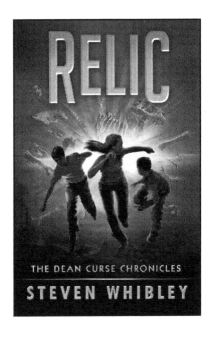

Fourteen-year-old Dean Curse is still having horrifying visions of the soon-to-be-dead. But after saving his sister, he sees it for the gift the mysterious society intended it to be.

So far, Dean's ability has cost him a few broken bones and a standing appointment at group therapy. But those are small sacrifices compared to the lives he's saved. But now, Dean – and his best friends, Colin and Lisa – are forced to make hard decisions that could get them in serious trouble with the law. They have less than twenty-four hours to decide if a few wrongs really can make a right.

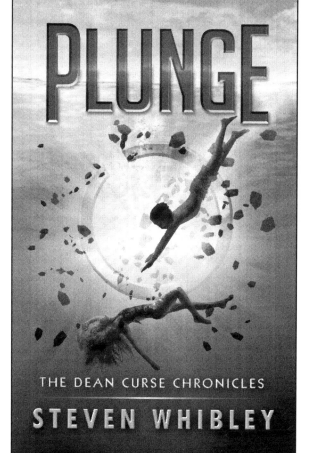

PLUNGE

THE DEAN CURSE CHRONICLES

STEVEN WHIBLEY

BOOK 4

RELEASE DATE TO BE ANNOUNCED

VISIT:

WWW.STEVENWHIBLEY.COM

ABOUT THE AUTHOR

Steven Whibley is the author of several middle grade and young adult novels. He lives in British Columbia with his wife and two young children. If you would like to connect with Steven, please check out his website at www.StevenWhibley.com

Made in the USA
San Bernardino, CA
28 May 2017